THE
NERDY DOZEN

JEFF MILLER

THE NERDY DOZEN

HARPER

An Imprint of HarperCollinsPublishers

alloyentertainment
Produced by Alloy Entertainment
1700 Broadway, New York, NY 10019

Design by Liz Dresner

Library of Congress Control Number: 2013951081

ISBN 978-0-06-227262-1

14 15 16 17 18   CG/RRDH   10 9 8 7 6 5 4 3 2 1
❖
First Edition

To Mom and Dad—for, well, pretty much everything

THE
NERDY DOZEN

CHAPTER 1

THE ENEMY FIGHTER JETS SURGED PAST NEIL ANDERTOL, soaring over desolate, sandy terrain. Neil glanced out either side of his cockpit window. Two planes from his own squad were flying parallel to his.

"Those our last ones?" Neil asked.

"Roger," said the pilot to his right. "They took out our other guys. It's just us three now."

Neil firmed his grip on the flight controls, his wiry hands confident. The small rocks on the ground had turned into boulders, and the boulders were giving way to vast cliffs. One of his fellow pilots passed Neil, swooping down toward the enemy planes.

"Be careful, man, it's danger—" Neil warned, but stopped as the fighter jet crashed into the side of a rock formation. A flash of orange and red reached for his cockpit's glass window like a fiery hand, warming the steel bottom of his jet.

The enemy planes rocketed forward. Ahead of them loomed the opening of a vast canyon.

"Shooter," Neil said into his headset to his only remaining ally, "there isn't enough space in that canyon for both of us."

The pilot, ShooterSam, shot Neil a thumbs-up and peeled away from behind Neil, barely clearing the canyon's dusty rim. "I got the bogey that followed me; you've got the other, right? Or do you need me to do all your work for you?" ribbed the voice in Neil's headset.

"Hey, let's not forget all those times I had to save you," Neil replied with a grin. The two pilots had flown together nearly every day for months, and apart from the competitive jabs, they were great friends.

Neil dived into the canyon below, closing in on the enemy fighter, sending a splash of rocks tumbling toward the small river below. He strained to set his automated target lock. The blinking icon of the enemy jumped up and down on Neil's radar screen. Neil shot through the sandstone canyon, steering dangerously close to the walls, but he couldn't stick with the bogey. The enemy plane increased in speed and began to pull away.

Time to do this the old-fashioned way, Neil thought. He disengaged the targeting system and took manual aim himself. He closed his left eye, aimed, and fired a rocket specifically designed to bring down an enemy intact—this time glancing off the enemy plane's right wing.

I've got 'em where I want 'em.

"Neil," said a voice behind him.

Neil ignored the interruption. He squinted through the fresh billows of smoke and leaned forward, sensing victory.

"Neil, are you *listening*?"

Neil's finger was wrapped around the controls. Just a few yards closer and he'd have completed the mission, securing the safety of his country. He could almost hear the roar of the crowd welcoming him home from the mission.

"Neil Andertol!" bellowed the voice. Neil

concentrated on the hum of his aircraft and the rhythmic beeping of his missile targeting system. He positioned himself directly behind the enemy jet and locked onto his target.

"Three, two—"

Then, suddenly, everything went black.

Neil ripped his headset off his mess of black hair and threw it on the ground.

"*Mom!* That's the farthest I've ever been! *Plus* I was about to save America, and a little bit of Nova Scotia!" he cried, glaring at the woman responsible for his abrupt demise. "I don't barge in during *Dr. Phil* right when some weirdo has a breakdown!"

Neil's mom dropped the unplugged television power cord to the floor and strode past him to the window. She yanked the blinds open, smiling as sunlight poured into her son's bedroom.

"At least those 'weirdos' don't sit in complete darkness on a beautiful Friday afternoon," she replied. Neil held his hands in front of his face, the glare of the sun slipping between his fingers. "Honey, it looks like wild animals live here." His mom gestured to the dirty towels, socks, and underwear littering the floor. She had a point—between Neil's suspicious hygiene habits and his aversion to natural light, his room could easily pass for the habitat of a nocturnal beast. Mrs. Andertol began to hum as she picked up dirty clothes.

Neil plugged the television back in and stared at the score from his recently ended game of Chameleon, which was his favorite online video game—and rumored to be a leaked military simulator. He gasped aloud when he saw the number flashing on the screen. Even with his sudden death at the end of the game, his score was the best he'd ever achieved.

"Come on, come on," Neil muttered under his breath, clicking frantically over to the game's main page. Neil had been in the number-two spot for weeks now, and no matter what he did, he couldn't seem to beat the worldwide champion.

"Nooo!" he moaned when the page loaded. There he was, ManofNeil, still listed underneath his nemesis, B4rrelR0ll. Neil's mom didn't even flinch as he banged the controller against the ground in frustration.

Neil brushed his hair to the side and stared intently at the TV screen, reading through the previous game's stats. Recently, rumors had been brewing online that after a player reached a certain high score, a feature unlocked that allowed the plane to go completely invisible. Neil wasn't sure he believed it, but just yesterday B4rrelR0ll had been bragging in all the forums that he'd finally done it. Neil winced at how close he'd come. ShooterSam's faint voice still chirped from the headset at his feet, but Neil didn't feel much like talking.

Sighing, Neil left Chameleon's home page and returned to the gaming lobby of his favorite site, Internet Piraseas. It was a site created for kids, by kids—or rather, by one kid in particular, thirteen-year-old hacker genius Reboot Robiski. No one knew the whereabouts of Reboot, who updated his site constantly. Neil had heard everything from a yacht cruising international waters to a yurt in Alaska to a presidential gaming cave below the White House.

Reboot's site was shrouded in mystery and extremely exclusive. To make sure only the best kids competed, Reboot required would-be members to create a GIF file, crack the top twenty scores worldwide in a game of their choice, and play for eleven uninterrupted hours. Neil had been a member for several years now, and he loved it. The most talented and competitive players were all here, and the site had a lot of games, like Chameleon, that couldn't be found anywhere else. Sometimes Neil wondered if Reboot himself ever played, but if he did, he probably did it in secret.

"Don't even think about turning that back on." Neil's mom stooped to pick up a dark-brown sweatshirt. "I've got big plans for you tonight."

Neil rolled his eyes. To him, "big plans" involved video games, a movie about video games, or a combination of the two, with the added element of pizza. To his mother, however, "big plans" consisted of museums, community theater, or something involving too much fresh air.

"But it's Friday! The Friday of a long weekend! So technically that's kind of like a double Friday! When else can I stay in my room for, like, sixty uninterrupted hours?" Neil sat cross-legged in his old corduroy chair, wearing well-worn shoes and faded jeans peppered with the crumbs of various snack foods. He was thin and wiry, and swimming in a new, way-too-large black T-shirt his mom had recently bought him.

"Your early twenties," Mrs. Andertol replied to her thirteen-year-old son, her eyes calculating which messy corner to tackle next. "Tonight we're all going to Colorado Springs for Janey's Memorial Day karate tournament."

Despite her sweet smile and innocent demeanor, Neil's eight-year-old sister, Janey, was frighteningly skilled in martial arts. She returned from each of these weekend tournaments with even more medals to add to the dozens already covering her bedroom walls.

In fact, her walls were so crowded that recently, Janey had started moving her bigger trophies to the mantel above the family's fireplace, which had a photo of Janey on one end and Neil on the other. Now that Janey's side was covered in shiny yellow-belt victories, Neil had scrambled to find things to decorate his end of the mantel. So far, all he had was a "Golden Floss" award from his dentist and the framed scorecard from a recent laser-tag victory.

But the worst part of Janey's training was that she seemed to think Neil was her living, breathing practice dummy. She regularly unleashed flurries of karate chops and roundhouse kicks on him at a moment's notice, in shopping malls, restaurant buffets, and farmer's markets. Nowhere was safe. Neil walked through grocery stores like a defensive ninja, constantly ready for a sneak attack in the frozen-foods section.

--

"Can't I just stay home?" Neil pleaded. "Or what's dad doing? He's not going, is he?"

"You know your father's away on-site for business for ten more days," she answered. "And you can't stay home alone, but that's what I'm getting to, honey. I know you don't want to be dragged along to another one of these things—"

"So I get to stay at Tyler's place?" In terms of real-life friends, Tyler was Neil's best. They'd met on Neil's first day of fourth grade three years ago, after Neil's family moved across Colorado. While waiting for their measles shots, they had bonded over a shared interest in video games—that and the fact that they'd both had the idea of hiding opened ketchup packets in their sleeves to freak out the school nurse. Now they were best friends, and banned for life from the nurse's office.

"No, Tyler and his family are at his grandma's for the weekend. But I talked to Mrs. Scott, and Tommy's having a weekend sleepover for all the boys with karate sisters who don't want to go. I said you'd join them." Her face peeked over the mountain of soiled linens. "Won't that be fun?"

"First off, I'm old enough to legally emancipate myself in Manitoba, so there's no *way* I am going to a sleepover my mother has organized," Neil said defensively. The only thing worse than enduring a beating from his kid sister was the prospect of facing Tommy Scott.

In Neil's first week at his new school, Tommy had hit Neil so hard with a kickball that Neil had doubled over, wheezing and moaning in full view of the entire playground. And in a terrible twist of fate, that very day, Miss Toll's science lesson had focused on Neanderthals, the early human ancestors who communicated with loud grunting noises and wild gestures. Gestures like the ones Neil demonstrated for students, teachers, and every-one else in view or earshot of the playground. From then on, thanks to Tommy, the name Neil Andertol died, and "Neandertol" was born.

"Who do you know in Manitoba?" Mrs. Andertol asked calmly, opening the closet door to fill his hamper.

"I read it online, but that's not the point!" Almost instinctively, Neil cleared his throat and quickly licked his palms to make them feel clammy. "Actually, I should probably just stay home this weekend. I'll be fine alone."

"Oh yeah?" she replied.

"Yeah," he answered. "I'm not feeling too good."

As an experienced professional in the art of faking

sick, Neil knew exactly what would happen next. He would lay the initial groundwork, his mother would express skepticism, and finally, with hard evidence, he would manage to convince her. Years ago, his mother had trusted him enough to take his word for it, but now he needed incontestable proof.

Neil's eyes darted around his room in search of something warm to hold up to his forehead. In his experience, the best fever simulators were sixty-watt lightbulbs. The worst was his mother's curling iron; the scalding metal had left him with nothing but a burn mark and three hours of waiting in the doctor's office.

"Well, if you're sick, you'll absolutely have to come with us," his mother called out from his closet. "They've got a top-notch infirmary at these karate weekends. I'm sure they'll be happy to cure you."

Beyond his closed bedroom door, Neil heard a loud, forceful "Hi-ya!" come from Janey downstairs.

"I think she just graduated to breaking wooden boards," Neil's mom added, stepping carefully out of the swamp that was Neil's closet and opening the door to the hallway.

Neil contemplated his two choices. Which was

worse, Tommy Scott or his terror of a sister? He froze as he heard a second howl from Janey, followed by the splintering crack of her hand breaking through pine. He imagined the board being his shoulder blade and almost felt a phantom pain.

"That better not be my new cutting board!" Neil's mom yelled down the stairs. She paused in Neil's doorway, her arms full of clothes. "I'd suggest you pack a bag for the weekend," she said. "I'm sure you'll have a great time."

CHAPTER

2

NEIL PRESSED HIS HEAD AGAINST THE GLASS OF THE BACK-seat window of his mom's station wagon. Inside his dark-green backpack were a few changes of clothes, various portable video-game devices, a fistful of gluten-free granola bars forced on him by his mother, and sour gummy worms he'd sneaked in for himself. He planned on avoiding human contact for the three-night span, and this was his survival kit.

"Neil, honey"—Mrs. Andertol turned to face him from the driver's seat—"you almost forgot these." She tossed back a light-blue toothbrush, a tube of toothpaste, and Neil's nighttime orthodontic headgear.

"But, Mom—" Neil started to protest, but his mother cut him off.

"No *buts*. Dr. Mullins said an overbite can come back in just one night," she said firmly. "When I was your age, I had to sleep with a back brace, and I still had lots of fun at sleepovers."

"That's because you didn't have electricity in medieval times and nobody could see you," Neil countered. "Things are different now. Charlie Jones came to school with crutches one day, and they sent him back a grade! I'm not wearing this thing."

"Charlie Jones failed social studies twice and has vertigo. You're wearing it, and that's final."

"'And that's final!'" mimicked Janey, who drove a fist into Neil's shoulder.

"Ow! Dear lord, do you file down your knuckles? They're, like, little bony daggers!" Neil glared at his sister before shoving the toothbrush and toothpaste into his bag's remaining space. Then he carefully dropped the headgear to the floor and nudged it just under his mother's front seat. He leaned back and turned his gaze outside again. He imagined piloting a fighter jet next to the car, swooping above the black SUV in the other lane.

"Maybe you could talk to Tommy about playing lacrosse with him and the other boys in the neighborhood," continued Neil's mom. "I'm sure they'd love to have somebody else on the team."

She went on, but Neil tuned her out. He was busy weaving in and out of the trees with his favorite copilot, ShooterSam. Even though they were best friends, they'd never met outside of a video game, and he didn't actually know his last name. For a brief moment, Neil entertained the fantasy that Sam's last name was secretly Scott, and he'd be at the sleepover, too.

"Let's go have some fun!" cheered Neil's mother as the Andertols' station wagon turned onto Tommy's driveway.

Dejected, Neil grabbed his bag and shuffled out of the car behind his mother. They walked over fake stones in a sea of aromatic fresh mulch. He turned to watch the shiny rims of the same black SUV he'd seen earlier slowly roll by, this time in the opposite direction. *They must be lost*, Neil thought. His housing development was seriously hard to navigate. Neil's mom turned his face toward her and rubbed a smudge of Doritos from the corner of his mouth and then rang the doorbell.

"*Mooom*," Neil whined as the front door opened.

"Jenny, good to see you!" Tommy's mom exclaimed, stepping back through the doorway. "Maggie's putting on her shoes, and then we'll be ready to go. Neil, the guys are downstairs—my oldest, Ted, will be in charge for this wacky boys' weekend! You like pizza?"

"Way more than your son," Neil mumbled.

"What was that, honey?" Mrs. Scott asked.

"Way more than some. I *love* pizza," Neal said sarcastically after getting an elbow from his mother.

"Well, it should be here pretty soon." She shut the door and headed toward the kitchen, chatting with Mrs. Andertol as she went.

Even though Neil had never been in Tommy's house, it felt familiar. The houses in their neighborhood were all built simultaneously, so everything—from the clean white kitchen floors to the cherry cabinets and soft tan carpet—was identical. Some houses even had the same layout.

Neil paused at the basement door, his hand on the brass knob, then took a deep breath and pushed it open.

The faint sound of laughter and explosions crept up the staircase. He slowly plodded downstairs, the thick carpet absorbing the sound of his footsteps.

In the basement, a group of boys was huddled on couches, facing a massive flat-screen TV. The light from the TV flickered over Tommy, who was standing in front, clutching the controller for dear life and frowning in concentration. The other boys shoveled cheesy orange popcorn into their mouths as they watched him play.

Neil quietly inched along the back wall, noting the faces illuminated by flashes of blue and red. Two of them happened to be the same face: the Stephens twins, neighborhood kids who did whatever Tommy told them. Next to them sat Jake Smith and Ron Goode, athletes with buzz cuts who had stolen upward of eighty-five dollars in lunch money from Neil over the past few years.

None of them noticed Neil come in. Their collective focus was on Tommy, all watching as he flew a jet fighter over vast mountains and lush forests, shooting floating pinecones for extra points.

Neil recognized the landscape instantly. Tommy was playing Chameleon, the very game Neil's mom had unplugged earlier that day. A wave of shock flooded through Neil. How had Tommy passed Reboot's entry exams to the site? Maybe he'd bullied someone else into passing them for him. After all, his skills looked pretty unimpressive.

"Nice shot," said one of the twins.

"Yeah, nice shot," followed the next.

It was, in fact, an awful shot. The ever-present threat of Tommy's thick fists tended to make his friends complimentary.

Neil's fingers grasped at an invisible controller, instinctively correcting Tommy's mistakes. He inched toward the television. Suddenly the overhead track lighting burst on, illuminating the basement in a wash of hundred-watt bulbs.

Squinting like video-game vampires, Tommy and company looked up at the lights, then directly at Neil.

"I didn't know you allowed cavemen in your house, Tommy," said Ron. The Stephens twins high-fived.

Neil looked down at the floor, biting his tongue on a comeback and hoping for some sort of lightning strike or natural disaster so he could go home.

Just then, a lumbering body came down the stairs, taking each step with a loud thump. It was Tommy's brother, Ted. Ted was a fatter, bearded, nineteen-year-old version of Tommy with more muscle and fewer brain cells. He lived at home and worked part-time as the Zamboni driver at a local ice rink. His reputation as a high school bully was legendary. It was said that he once made the captain of the chess team eat a rook.

Neil's eyes locked onto a stack of board games on a table beneath the stairs. He cringed at the white-and-red Monopoly box, imagining a hotel in his lower intestine. No passing Go. No collecting two hundred dollars. Some real Baltic Avenue–style pain.

"Which one of you is Neil?" Ted asked.

"I think you mean Neandertol," Tommy corrected. "That's him."

Neil braced himself for the oncoming torture. Maybe he could lobby for a less-threatening board game, something along the lines of Connect Four or Sorry!

"Your mom told me to give this to you. She said you, like, forgot this in the car or something," Ted said, brandishing the metal monster Neil had attempted to leave under his mother's seat. "I think your sister found it."

Neil felt all the blood rush out of the upper third of his body. Public exposure of unsightly orthodontic hardware was enough to send a kid into homeschooling or, at the very least, into transferring school districts. And now his was being flaunted for everyone to see.

"Is that supposed to help you stop grunting, Neandertol?" Jake said with a laugh.

Neil stuffed the headgear into his backpack and turned to follow Ted upstairs. He hoped maybe his mom was still in the driveway. Being Janey's punching bag for the weekend was clearly now the lesser of two evils.

"Where ya goin', Neandertol? It's your turn to play." Tommy's voice stopped him in his tracks. Neil knew Tommy wasn't sharing for generosity's sake—he wanted Neil to embarrass himself even further. "Or would you rather make some spears and go looking for masterdons?"

"They're called mastodons," Neil murmured.

"What?" Tommy challenged.

"Mastodons. They're called mastodons," Neil said louder.

"Whatever. Here you go, caveman," said Tommy, tossing him the controller. "This should be good—Neandertol is still figuring out the wheel."

Tommy fell backward onto a couch, sniggering with the others beside him. Neil took the controller in his hands and curled his fingers around the joystick

The game began, and Neil set off. He effortlessly escaped from enemy fighters, weaving back and forth to dodge rocket-propelled grenades. Neil knew every detail of the level, and it showed. He flew through the crossfire, nearly unscathed by the explosions around him.

A hush descended over the boys on the couches. Five minutes later Neil had eclipsed Tommy's high score. And he was just getting started.

After Neil pulled off a particularly impressive barrel roll, Jake broke the silence looming over the basement. "Man . . . you're really good."

"Yeah," the twins said softly, mesmerized by the glowing flat screen.

When the level came to an end, Neil had almost tripled the current high score. Tommy stewed on the couch, his gray eyes brimming with fury.

"Whoa, that was awesome. Neil, how long have you played this?" said Ron.

"Umm, for a few months, I guess," Neil replied. "It's a fun game."

"You gotta teach us some of that stuff," begged one of the twins. "How did you do that barrel roll thing?"

"Oh, it's easy, actually. You guys could do it for sure," Neil responded.

The doorbell sent everyone flying off the couches in search of pizza.

"Neil, once we eat, we're watching you again," Jake said as he rushed upstairs. "That was awesome."

Neil smiled and set the controller down next to the television. Maybe his mom was right after all. This weekend might actually be fun.

Tommy was the only one still in the basement. "Nice job," he said, his voice dangerously low.

"Thanks," Neil muttered, slipping around him.

"Oh, Neandertol, one more thing . . ."

"Yeah?" Neil turned, only to catch Tommy's fist swinging into his stomach, knocking the wind out of him. Neil dropped to one knee, bracing himself on a small end table as he gasped for air.

"Looks like in real life you're still a loser." On his way to the stairs, Tommy noticed Neil's backpack half open against the wall. Smiling maliciously, he held his foot over the bag and stomped it with a sickening crunch.

"Oops." He smirked.

Then he ran upstairs, taking the steps two at a time.

Neil walked over slowly to survey the damage, clutching his stomach. Peeling back the zipper, he saw what he feared most—chunks of headgear littering his bag.

Sighing, he slung the backpack over his shoulder and crept upstairs to peer out the basement doorway. The hallway was empty. He eyed a sliding glass door across from him and edged toward it, pausing once he'd opened it partway. Tommy and the others were in the kitchen.

Neil wasn't sure what kind of trouble he'd get into for leaving the sleepover so early, or what Tommy's brother would tell his mom when he realized Neil was missing. Maybe, Neil hoped, he wouldn't say anything. As Neil stood there wondering how he could survive three days alone and what kinds of punishment he could expect on Monday, he distinctly heard the words *veggie pizza*.

Well, that seals the deal. Neil shrugged and slipped out into the dark night.

CHAPTER

3

A LIGHT RAIN HAD FALLEN, LEAVING THE AIR HEAVY AND moist under a sliver of moon. Neil's shoes flicked water onto the black asphalt of the street as he hurried away from Tommy's house.

Under a buzzing streetlight, he adjusted his backpack, groaning at the sounds of the expensive headgear confetti shifting back and forth at the bottom of his bag. What could he possibly tell his mom when she returned from Janey's competition on Monday?

The backpack was ravaged by wild animals. . . . There

was a science mishap. . . . You see, there's a secret organization of crooked-teeth enthusiasts. . . . His mother would see right through any of these, but the truth was out of the question. Tommy had cultivated an angelic reputation among the neighborhood's mothers, thanks to his habit of calling them "ma'am" and a thorough knowledge of household uses for Coca-Cola. He was untouchable.

Neil walked slowly, dodging earthworms that had crept up during the rain. The roads were empty, with only the sound of crickets filling the night air. Neil's head bobbed with his gangly strides. His shoes scuffed and scraped the street as he kicked at a small rock.

With his mom at his sister's competition, Neil had three days to develop a believable story. But it would need to be foolproof. While most of his mother's punishments revolved around chores and forced outdoor time, something this bad might push her to ban all electronics from Neil's life. A fate worse than death. Neil wondered how far it was to Tyler's grandma's house. Tyler could at least help him come up with a believable excuse.

Neil rounded the corner to his street as a pair of headlights appeared behind him. He veered to the right, leaving space for the car to pass. Neil was just starting to contemplate the phenomenon of "orthodontic heat lightning" when he realized that the car was still rolling ten yards behind him. Neil turned to his left and waved for the vehicle to go by, shuffling sideways.

The car came to a stop, its headlights fixed firmly on Neil, bright and blinding.

"Neil Andertol?" boomed a voice. The driver's-side door opened.

"Tommy? Ted?" Neil said to the two shadowy outlines.

Silence. Neil had a bad feeling it wasn't Tommy and his meathead brother.

"Afraid not." One of the shadows spoke, starting to move forward. "We need you to come with us, son."

No way. Neil immediately pulled down on his backpack straps, took a breath, and started to run, keeping his eyes locked on his house in the distance. The dim yellow light above his garage beckoned invitingly. For the first time outside gym class, Neil sprinted as fast as he possibly could. The balls of his feet flew across the still-wet pavement.

He had gone only a few yards when strong hands grabbed his arms and legs from behind, hoisting him up as he thrashed in the air.

"What's going on? Who are you?" Neil shouted, kicking wildly.

"We're with the government," said the man holding his flailing legs. He nodded toward a badge attached to his leather belt. Neil didn't know what it was for, but it looked official.

"Tommy broke it! I swear Tommy broke my head-gear! It's not my fault!" Neil screamed.

They carried Neil toward a sleek black SUV, where another figure was waiting with a giant sack. Under the fuzzy light of the moon Neil could see it was the same SUV he'd seen earlier, and his assailants were uniformly dressed in camouflage.

This, Neil realized, was not about his headgear.

The uniforms were the last thing he saw before the bag was pulled over his head and he was stuffed into the backseat. His heart racing, Neil struggled to free himself from the black bag, but then he felt the sting of a needle in his thigh and knew it was too late. His eyelids grew heavy as everything faded into darkness.

★ ★ ★

Neil woke up slowly. He felt groggy, and his head hurt. He peeled himself up from the dark wooden bench he was lying on and ran his hands through his hair, blinking in confusion at his surroundings.

Eleven other kids were also sitting on benches, which skirted the perimeter of a rectangular cinder-block room. A boy about Neil's age jumped up and walked to the room's only door, yanking unsuccessfully at its huge silver handle. He finally kicked the base of the door in frustration.

"You have no idea how much trouble you're going to be in when my dad is through with you!" the boy yelled at the door. He had speckled green eyes and a jutting jaw beneath short, reddish-blond hair. "I hope you like prison!" He paused for a response, his nostrils flaring, but was met with only silence. Finally he gave the door one more kick for good measure and slumped back on a bench, crossing his arms sullenly.

"You really showed that door who's boss" came a scratchy voice from a corner. Neil looked to see who said it, but his eyes were still foggy. No one laughed as eleven sets of eyes moved from the door to the infuriated redhead and back.

For the most part, the other dazed kids looked about Neil's age, too, except for a scrawny boy in the corner, who couldn't have been older than ten. Neil wondered if everyone else had ended up here the same way he had— the ominous strongmen, the bag, the roadside grab. He turned to the boy on his right, who had long, unwashed brown hair and crooked metal-framed glasses. His lenses, the kind designed to transition between the outdoors and indoors, seemed stuck somewhere in between.

"Do you know what's going on here?" Neil whispered. The boy turned to Neil. He shook his head and took a deep puff from an inhaler.

"As always, the dice will tell us," the boy said, pulling a twenty-sided die from his pocket. Neil was puzzled.

"Do these dice . . . talk to you?" Neil asked. He watched as the boy rolled it on the polished finish of the slatted wooden bench. It finally came to a stop, showing a 3.

"Things could be better. But we will get answers soon."

"You got all that from a three?"

"Yes. But do not worry. I just leveled up with my dungeon master to become an expert-grade elf archer/ blacksmith. I'm Yuri the Long-Toothed," the boy replied, extending a clammy hand. "Or just Yuri, for short." In his other hand was another twenty-sided die, its smooth edges rolling around in his palm.

"Oh. Um, cool," Neil said. "I'm Neil. I'm not much of an archer or a blacksmith, but I did get kicked out of shop class for making sawdust angels, if that helps."

Yuri started to respond, but whatever he was about to say was interrupted by the loud scrape of a deadbolt.

Everyone turned toward the door, which opened inward slowly to reveal a distinguished-looking gentleman in an Air Force uniform. He was tall, with buzzed hair that was more gray than brown. Neil would have known even without his endless rows of medals that he was a top-ranking official.

"My dad is going to destroy you!" the redhead shouted, jumping up from his seat.

"You must be Trevor," the man said, reading a name from his manifest and shooting the boy a glance that halted him in his tracks. "I am Major—"

"I have a right to a phone call!" Trevor shouted. "One phone call, and I'll have the best lawyer in Massachusetts all over your—"

"Son, if you'll give me a minute, I will explain what's going on," the major interrupted. "I am Air Force Major

Jones. You have all been brought here for an important mission."

Neil looked around the room at the others, letting the major's words sink in. He swallowed hard. *Air Force? What could they want from me?*

"I do apologize for the, shall we say, *aggressive* method of recruitment," Jones went on. "But time is not a luxury we can afford at the moment. Now, if you'll all follow me." He turned abruptly and opened the door, leaving the kids to scramble behind him.

At first no one moved. Then a girl—the only girl, Neil realized—jumped up from one of the corners, her dark-brown hair bobbing from side to side, and hurried out after the major. One by one, the others in the room did the same. Neil followed Yuri after he'd rolled 11 three consecutive times.

Neil walked down the hall in silence, stealing occasional glances at the rest of the group. The shiny granite floor chirped with each step, a squeaky symphony bouncing off the light fixtures on each wall. When they finally reached the end of the hallway, the major slid open a heavy metal door, revealing a massive hangar illuminated by bright white lights.

"*This* is why you are here," he announced, stepping back and clasping his arms firmly behind his back. The group shuffled in, their eyes scanning the vast room. But there was nothing to see. The hangar was completely empty.

NEIL FILED INTO THE ROOM AND STOOD AT THE END OF THE row of kids. He could feel his heart beating in his ears and the sweat building on his brow. Without warning, one of the kids took off at a sprint toward the glowing EXIT sign at the far end of the hangar, knocking Neil off balance. The *pop* of the boy's sneakers rang loudly in the empty space. Then out of nowhere, when he wasn't even halfway across the room, he slammed to the floor, as if he'd been thrown back by some invisible obstacle. He lay there for a few moments, then sat up slowly, wincing and rubbing his head. No one moved toward him as he crawled back to the group.

"Ahem." Jones cleared his throat loudly, ignoring the stunned boy. "A-*tten*-tion!"

A few kids attempted to snap up straight and tall, but the effect was messy and amateurish. The major rolled his eyes and yelled even louder.

"Maybe you didn't hear me. I said, a-*tten*-tion!" he barked. It was obvious he wasn't used to repeating his orders.

This time, Neil snapped upright, his hand forming a straight line above his brow. The rest of the others did something similar, but it was still far from perfect. They looked more like a lineup camping outside a store for a new video game than soldiers.

"Soldiers," the major began, then paused. He seemed uncomfortable calling the kids before him "soldiers."

"Recruits, I'd like to introduce you all to the CTM-30." He nodded to a set of windows on the right side of the hangar, where soldiers wearing headsets sat behind control decks.

Suddenly, in the center of the vast room, the outline of a sleek fighter jet shimmered into view. Neil watched spellbound as it became more defined, revealing its sharp contours and perfectly aerodynamic wingspan. He didn't have to look around at the rest of the group to know that they were as shocked as he was.

Jones nodded at the now-visible fighter jet and then back to his lineup. "It can reach speeds as high as Mach four, has an operating altitude higher than one hundred thousand feet, boasts a thrust-to-weight ratio that will make your head spin, and can go completely invisible at the touch of a button. Only a select few even know it exists." He paused. "Or its nickname: the Chameleon."

Neil grew pale.

Now it all made sense: the kidnapping, the base, the imposing major. He had been caught playing a pirated military simulator and was here to pay for his crimes. But even in the midst of his panic, he couldn't help feeling a bit of awe. This plane was the one he'd been piloting six hours a day, sometimes ten on weekends—and it was real, very, very real. It actually went *invisible*.

So if I'm here for the game . . . that must mean everybody else here is. . . . He peered down the line, wondering if Sam might have made the cut, but realized that he had no idea what his friend looked like.

"Now, before anyone else decides to make another run for the door, you need to know you're not in trouble," Jones began.

"Ten hours ago, the only operational plane of this kind departed on its very first mission, piloted by the only two people trained to fly it. They took off from an aircraft carrier in the western Pacific and went down far from the mission target, somewhere at sea.

"We've detected the plane's distress signal, which sends off coordinates as well as an electromagnetic pulse to deactivate bogeys in the area, but unfortunately, it cut out the pilots' communication in the process. We have reason to believe, though, that both pilots have survived, but they could be in grave danger. And of course, we cannot afford to let anyone else find the Chameleon. The invisibility technology must not fall into the wrong hands."

Neil imagined the Chameleon floating on the surface of the ocean, like an invisible reptilian pool toy.

"The mission we've planned consists of a rescue and retrieval of the pilots and the aircraft," Jones continued.

In front of Neil, the boy who'd tried to make a dash out of the hangar shot up his hand with a question.

The major turned his attention to him and glared. The boy, looking more confused by the second, slowly dropped his hand.

"The ideal plan of attack," Jones explained, "would have been to send in another Chameleon with a trained military flight crew, since the only way to see an invisible Chameleon is in the cockpit of another. But while we have three more of these advanced aircraft, as I said, the only pilots with enough flight hours logged are now MIA."

Is there good news with this? Neil wondered.

"However, it came to my attention this afternoon that the Chameleon's flight simulator made it onto the internet." The major began to pace. "So, even though you are all in direct violation of at least six codes dealing with classified military intel"—the major frowned—"whether I like it or not, it seems that civilians with video-game experience are the only people in the world with adequate training to fly these things. And you all represent the twelve best."

Neil lifted his eyes and met the major's stare.

"I'm here with a challenge to you all. Bring our men home."

A loudspeaker overhead crackled to life. "Sir,

permission to speak with you for a moment?"

The major nodded and headed toward the control room, leaving the motley group to absorb his words.

Neil exhaled and relaxed his shoulders and neck, taking a few steps toward the pristine fighter jet. He slid his hand up the front of the plane and felt the cool metal beneath his fingertips.

"It's like something out of a movie, right?" said a voice behind him. Neil turned to see a fellow recruit, nearly a foot taller and maybe a year older. Shaggy brown hair poked out from under a baseball cap that said RECYCLING! in silver lettering.

"Hey, man, the name's Biggs," the boy said, holding out his hand. Neil noticed that his arm was covered with hemp bracelets and what looked like scratches from cats. He wore a faded blue T-shirt and fraying corduroys. He reminded Neil of the kids who met outside school every day to play hacky sack.

"Neil," Neil said, shaking Biggs's hand.

The two stood in silence for a moment, taking it all in, and then began to walk around the side of the jet, trailing their hands along its edges in amazement. The plane was shaped like a sleek Y, with a glass cockpit in the center and two turbine engines at its rear. Mesmerized by the jet, they almost collided with the lone girl Neil had seen earlier, who was circling the plane in the opposite direction. She was wearing denim pants and an orange plaid shirt over a white tee. Wisps of brown hair escaped her rubber-banded pigtails to frame her oval-shaped face.

"Hey, I'm Samantha," she said in a scratchy voice that sounded weirdly familiar. She had big brown eyes and a smile that pulled up at the corners of her mouth.

"Biggs," the other boy said.

Samantha looked over to Neil, but he just stood there blankly. Meeting strangers was one thing, but meeting strangers who were *girls* was entirely different. He prayed silently for another natural disaster to wipe out this awkward moment.

Flash flood! Tornado! Something, please!

"And this is Neil," Biggs added, giving him a nudge. Neil managed a quick hello and then turned back to the fighter jet, his pulse racing.

"Hi, Neil." Samantha squinted at him as though considering something.

Luckily for Neil, Jones chose that exact moment to reappear, saving him from any more uncomfortable silences. Now standing on either side of the major were two strong-looking soldiers.

"Cadets, I just had a discussion with my ranking officers"—he nodded to the muscular men—"and we've since received intelligence giving us a more precise location of the pilots, so we're going to move quickly. We will mobilize a rescue mission in no more than ten hours, and one of you will serve as pilot, with three others to assist in flight. Your training begins at oh-four-hundred hours."

Neil looked down at his watch. It was midnight. He'd been gone from Tommy's sleepover for only three hours maybe, but it felt like a whole day. He wondered if anybody was looking for him.

"The training will consist of a flight simulation and something we like to call the Decider," Jones explained. "Based on the results, the top three of you will be selected to staff an aircraft, which will be led by a specialized soldier. The rest of you will be sent home.

"That said, we do not have the right to hold you against your will, so if you want to leave, now is your chance. I'll have Captain Wells here escort you out personally."

Hesitantly, the boy who had tried to escape earlier raised his hand.

"Um . . . the only video game I've ever played involves digitally raising livestock. Am . . . am I in the right place?" he stammered. The major nodded to Wells, who led the kid out of the hangar, which left only eleven standing there.

For an instant Neil considered leaving, too. But what did he have to return to? An overbearing mom, broken headgear, a weekend of Tommy Scott, and physical intimidation by his little sister?

He'd rather take his chances with the Air Force.

CHAPTER

5

THE NEW RECRUITS SHUFFLED THROUGH QUIET CORRIDORS, led by Lopez, the second, and burlier, of Jones's two soldiers. He had chocolate-colored skin, buzzed hair, and forearms that could probably crack lobster claws. Or heads.

Neil did his best to stay in line with the others. From what he could tell, the building was shaped like a giant hexagon. The group walked down a large hallway and came across turns at the exact same angle every fifty steps or so. At every corner were corridors leading in two different directions, like small veins branching out from an artery. Neil craned his neck, trying to look down each one, wondering what kind of secrets it held.

As Neil pushed on a heavy door to peer into a room labeled MISSILE TARGETING CHAMBER, he heard a quick whistle. It was Lopez, who had slowed to halt at the hallway intersection. "This is the men's barracks," he said, pointing to the door on his right. "Ladies' is two doors down. Uniforms are on the bunks. Lights-out in fifteen minutes." He opened the door to the men's barracks, and the boys shuffled past. Neil looked back at Samantha, their eyes meeting for an instant before the door swung closed behind him.

The room was long, with six metal double-decker bunks lining the edges. Laid out on each bed was a camouflage uniform, accompanied by a pair of boots and a set of silvery dog tags.

"Whoa, look. They have our names on 'em," said a kid as everyone fanned out to look for his assigned bunk.

Neil found his tags on the bottom bunk of a bed in the corner. He rubbed his fingers over his name, now etched into stainless steel, and smiled, full of surprising confidence. Hours ago he would never have imagined himself wearing something this official, this *cool*. He looped the cold metal chain around his skinny neck. No matter what, he thought, he had to be the pilot chosen.

Even though the mattress looked thin and lumpy, Neil knew that he needed a few hours of sleep if he was going to have a chance of earning a spot the next day. With a yawn, he plopped down on the bed—only to feel the mattress slip out from beneath him.

"Oww!" Neil exclaimed as he hit the slats hard and bumped his head on the bed's frame.

Trevor, the hothead who had threatened legal action earlier, hovered over him.

"Scram, nerd." Trevor threw Neil's uniform at his chest. "This bunk's mine,"

"Uh, I think you're up top," Neil said, rubbing his head where he'd bumped it. He wasn't sure what right Trevor had calling anyone a nerd. Trevor had the kind of pale skin that hadn't seen the sun for so long that Neil could see the blue veins beneath it on the undersides of his forearms.

"Nah, my tags were on this one," Trevor replied. He tossed his tags next to where Neil sat. "See?"

"I got room over here, Neil," Biggs offered, pointing

to his bottom bunk. "I like sleeping closer to the ceiling. It helps me center my chi."

"Thanks." Neil had no clue what he was talking about, but he shuffled over to Biggs and sat down on the mattress. Trevor was still watching him from across the room.

"Hey, man, so I was thinking," Biggs said, hopping on one foot as he untied his shoes. "If we all got brought in here because we play Chameleon, does that make you ManofNeil?"

"Uh, yeah, actually," Neil said, smiling. It felt odd to hear his screen name in real life. "Wait, does that mean that—"

"Dude, that's awesome! I'm MrBiggShot! You're, like, a *legend*, man," Biggs gushed. "Although I thought maybe, you'd be, I don't know . . . more jacked." He laughed.

"Um, thanks, I guess." Neil blushed at the compliment. "You're really good, too. You beat me three times last weekend!"

"Thanks, man! I just can't believe I'm meeting you, ya know, face-to-face."

Biggs took a step on Neil's bed and rolled onto his own, the frame wiggling beneath his shifting weight.

As his legs swooped up, a small green notebook fell out of his pants pocket. "Hey, Biggs, you dropped this," Neil said, bending down and handing the notebook up to his bunkmate. The word *smells* was scrawled onto the front in black ink.

"Oh, thanks, man. Can't go anywhere without the smell journal."

"Without . . . what?"

Biggs leaned over the railing, his head bobbing above Neil like a shaggy-haired puppet. "I've got this sweet idea for—brace yourself—*smellable TV*. There could be a box below your TV, or a thing you attach to your phone, that emits chemicals, so when something comes on, like flowers, you actually smell the flowers. Or if you're watching baseball and a dude spills nachos all over himself trying to catch a ball, you smell the nachos, and the guy. Well, more so the nachos for now. I'm still working on dual smell-sations. But think of how awesome it would be if TV involved more than just two senses. It would be like going inside the TV!"

Neil raised his eyebrows. His bunkmate was either brilliant or insane. Possibly both.

"So I've got this bad boy with me at all times.

Whenever I smell something that I want in there, I write it down and see if I can re-create it. It's all about finding the right mix of chemicals. So far I've perfected over thirty smells," Biggs said proudly, patting the notebook.

"Lights-out, recruits!" a soldier barked from the doorway, and the overhead fluorescent lights turned off with a click. The soldiers here reminded Neil of the drill sergeants on reality shows, the ones who screamed at runaway teenagers or overweight celebrities.

Neil pulled back the covers on his bunk and slid in. "Well, I'll let you know if I smell anything good," he whispered.

"Thanks, man. I'm working on bacon right now." Biggs yawned, then rolled sideways with a massive squeak from the mattress. "I'm beat. Night, ManofNeil."

"Night, MrBiggShot. See you in the morning."

Neil closed his eyes and slowly traced his name on his dog tag with his thumb and forefinger, circling to a stop as he drifted into sleep.

★ ★ ★

The roar of the helicopter blades drowned out the roar of the crowd as Neil stepped from the chopper onto the football field. Squinting into the flashes of dozens of cameras, he looked around at the mass of people who'd come to welcome him home. He started toward the podium, where his parents and the mayor were waiting for him, his dozens of medals jangling with each step. They held a trophy that was the size of his family's mantel, maybe even bigger. He would have been able to fit all of Janey's awards into the sparkling cup.

As a slew of cheerleaders began to chant "N-E-I-L" and the band of twenty-seven electric guitars struck up a rock anthem, Neil waved to the crowd, soaking up the applause. A young child, her hair in platinum-blond pigtails, held a sign reading NEIL 4 PRESIDENT. A hush fell over everyone as he approached the podium's microphone.

"No, my king! The cooked goose has been poisoned!"

"What?" Neil looked around puzzled and scanned the crowd, but the band was starting up again, twanging loudly. He turned his attention back to the podium, but it was gone.

★ ★ ★

Neil groggily blinked awake to the sound of Biggs's mattress springs twanging against his weight. He turned to his right to see another recruit talking in his sleep. He was pudgy and was thrashing his stubby legs around in the rickety military-grade bunk.

"We must alert the others, my liege," the other boy continued, rolling over on his side and drifting back into silence.

Through the tiny, prison-sized window, Neil could see that it was still dark out. He looked down at his watch. Three a.m. He sat up, rubbed the sleep out of his eyes, and stretched his neck back and forth. The bunk bed was not particularly comfortable, but it sure beat sleeping on the floor of Tommy Scott's basement. Neil figured Tommy and his gang would probably have permanent-markered his face by now.

Ha, Neil laughed to himself as he looked down at the dog tags around his neck. *Tommy Scott will never get to do this.* Neil tucked the tags back beneath his undershirt but didn't lie back down. His T-shirt was sweaty, and his shaggy black hair clung to his forehead. A shower sounded like a good idea right now. And he didn't think he could go back to sleep after that dream anyway.

The tan linoleum was cool under Neil's bare feet as he tiptoed to the bathroom. Inside, he paused in front of the mirror to get a good look at himself. His brow furrowed. Something was out of place. Sure, he was a little skinny for an Air Force uniform, but it was more than that.

Then it hit him: the hair. He had never seen a soldier with any semblance of shaggy hair. Neil ran his hand through his thick mop and nodded at his reflection. The hair had to go.

Neil peered up at the slender metal shelf above the row of sinks where various grooming products were displayed. There was shaving cream but no razor. Neil scratched his head and spied a pair of scissors in the corner. *That will do*, he thought.

He grabbed a clump of hair and snipped away. Strands fell like ticker tape into the sink below. But Neil's adrenaline rush dissipated quickly as he started to realize just how time-intensive cutting his hair so short would be. He'd managed to trim off only a few inches above his right ear when his arms grew heavy and tired. His three a.m. wake-up was beginning to wear on him. *No pain, no gain*, Neil thought grimly; he started to snip on the left side, too.

Just as he'd cut a few more shreds to even his progress, Biggs burst through the bathroom door, fully dressed.

"Neil, there you are, man. We all overslept. And I

think I had a dream that Trevor changed your watch time. . . ." Biggs yawned. "Three minutes till we have to report to the mess hall, man," he said quickly as other recruits poured into the bathroom to use the facilities. "It's the second door on the right once you hang a ricky outta here. Hurry!" Biggs went back out the doorway.

Neil quickly ran back to his bed and threw on the camouflage pants, gray shirt, and shoes in record speed. Then he raced down the hall to face the most important day of his life.

CHAPTER

6

NEIL PUSHED THROUGH THE DOOR MARKED **MESS HALL** AND looked around for Biggs. The recruits this morning seemed even smaller than they had the night before, huddled together at a single table in a room that could easily accommodate hundreds. Neil ran to the buffet line, where a haphazard breakfast had been set out. He quickly chose a plain bagel, ripped it in half, and slathered a generous amount of cream cheese on each piece. He poured himself a glass of orange juice and slid into the spot across from Biggs.

It was only after he'd inhaled half his bagel that he looked up to see Biggs's curious expression.

"Neil . . . ," his bunkmate said slowly, "what happened to your hair?"

In his panic at possibly missing training, Neil had nearly forgotten all about his ill-fated haircut. He reached up nervously to the side of his head. Gulping, he grabbed a spoon to use as a makeshift mirror, but it only confirmed what he'd feared. His shaggy hair was now framed by two almost-bald patches, one of which was larger than the other, both slightly uneven.

"Nice hair," Trevor said with a smirk from a few seats down.

"Nah, it's not so bad. You've got this kind of . . . European thing going on. I can dig it." Biggs paused, then burst out laughing.

"'Tis a noble hair trimming indeed," said the boy next to Neil. It was the sleeptalker from before.

"Neil, this is Riley. Riley, my main man Neil," Biggs introduced.

"My lords," Riley said in an old-fashioned, most certainly fake British accent. He nodded, as if to pay respects.

"Riley does those Renaissance Faire things," Biggs explained. "Cool, huh?"

At that moment, Jones strode into the room, flanked by Wells and Lopez.

"A-*tten*-tion!" said Jones. His forehead was crinkled with age lines that arched toward his black-and-gray buzz cut. Neil could see the muscles on either side of the major's jaw bulging from gritted teeth. *That's got to be the thickest neck I've ever seen on a human*, he thought.

Everyone at Neil's table stood up quickly, knocking their chairs back in the process.

"Still needs some work," Jones said. His voice was gravelly and deep, like Neil's father's was when he would fall asleep watching sports and then try to act like he hadn't. "You'll be forming two groups, one of five and one of six. When I call your name, line up behind me here," Jones went on. "Second group, line up behind Lopez. My team will head to flight simulation. The rest of you will be joining Lopez and Wells for the physical component, the Decider. Then we'll switch." His eyes caught Neil's newly styled hair, and he paused.

"Okay, then," he said, and looked down at the paper in his hand.

"Samantha Elizabeth Gonzales." Samantha moved to stand behind Jones.

"Jason . . . ," Jones continued, as two boys started forward. "Oh, looks like we've got two. Both of you, then." Jones marked a check on the clipboard in his hands and continued with their names, but Neil's thoughts ran elsewhere.

Oh no, Neil panicked. *Not middle names.*

"Robert St . . ." Jones paused.

"Starlight. My parents had me on the solstice," Biggs said, grinning.

"Robert *Starlight* Hurbigg. Trevor Phillip Grunsten."

Please, please don't say my middle name.

"And finally, Neil Ashley Andertol."

"Yeah, that's me," Neil murmured as he studied the major's shoes. A small laugh rippled through a few in the group, but Trevor's was by far the loudest.

"It's a family name," Neil defended in a whisper. It was true—it had been passed down through generations from a grandfather with at least five *great*s. But why couldn't his mom have waited until Janey to use that particular name?

"Yeah, passed from your grandmother to all her daughters," Trevor muttered.

"Listen up, everybody," Jones cut in. "Before we head into training, I want to tell you the same thing I was told on my first day of combat drills." He cleared his throat and clasped his rough hands. "You're getting ready to climb a mountain, and it's not an easy one. It will be tough. You will be lonely. You will be exhausted. But you are representing your country, and if you want to be the best, you have to remember to keep climbing. And if you run into problems—well, don't come to me. I'm not in the business of babysitting. Now, let's move out!"

★ ★ ★

Neil and the five others in his group paused with Jones in front of a white door marked SIMULATION CHAMBER.

"Recruits," Jones began, "welcome to the first part of training. You'll find that this flight sim is quite similar to the game you've all been playing, just a little more . . . realistic." His eyes gleamed with excitement. "While the game you've been playing is more of a stripped-down version we'd planned to send to other bases, these babies have all the bells and whistles."

Neil imagined that "bells and whistles," in this case, most likely meant things ready and willing to give you whiplash. Inside the room, six massive boxes lowered to the ground with an eruption of hydraulic lifts and mechanical grinding. The doors slid open in unison, slowly displaying faintly illuminated cockpit seats. High-definition panels were visible in every direction, forming a glowing cocoon for the pilot.

In front of them loomed a jumbo high-definition screen, showing the video feed from the game's map and the individual flight simulators.

"Now, we'll be basing everything on time and score. There will be three separate rounds, twenty-five computer-generated enemy bogeys, and the six of you. The first two rounds will be cooperative, sort of like a capture-the-flag situation." Jones clicked a button on a small controller cradled in his fingers. "We call it man on fire."

"Ahem, person on fire, please," Biggs said, nodding in Sam's direction.

"Right. Person on fire. Basically, one teammate will have the 'flag,' which on your screen will look like the jet is engulfed in flames. Your job is to protect the jet, or make sure you're not taken down if you're the one on fire," Jones explained.

Everyone watched a simulated round on the screen, with one fighter in flames as teammates flew in formation to protect it.

"Second round puts you on the offensive. An AI bogey is your man on fire, and you've got to take 'em out. Since there are more of them than you, things should get interesting quick," Jones said. He clicked his control once more.

"Final round is every ma—sorry, every *person* for themselves against the computers. No time limit, most bogeys eliminated wins. And none of these 'extra lives' or whatever it is you kids have in these games. This is the real deal: when you're down, you're down. And when things start to go wrong, these simulators will make sure you know it. Any questions?" No one responded. "I said, any questions?"

"Sir, no, sir!" the group shouted back.

"That's more like it. Next time, don't make me ask twice. All right, double-time to the chambers."

"Ladies first, Ashley," Trevor said, pushing Neil to take the first simulation chamber.

Neil felt his ears flush. He'd spent years making sure no one knew his middle name, and it was the Air Force, somehow, that ended up giving it away.

"We'll see who's a lady when the scores are read,"

Neil said as he ducked inside the chamber.

"Hey, I can kick both your butts," Sam retorted, and pushed past Trevor, giving Neil a cold stare, too.

"Oh, right. Sorry," Neil mumbled.

Neil took a deep breath and fastened himself into the sturdy leather chair. The door closed, and air filled the hydraulic lifts beneath the machine as it rose off the ground. He secured his headset, which was much bigger and offered more padding than the flimsy one he was used to.

"We've entered first names into the system for scoring," Jones said. "Since we've got two Jasons, I'm calling you Jason One and Jason Two."

"I'm One!" said Jason 1 over his headset. "Sorry. I get a little competitive sometimes." Jason 2 made no effort at radio communication.

The array of levers, buttons, and instruments in front of Neil was overwhelming, but they seemed familiar. He quickly ran his hands over the control panel, testing various parts and getting to know the layout. It was just like the game, but better.

The control stick for the plane looked like a hybrid of a standard joystick and the video-game controller on Neil's gaming console. It required two hands, had a groove for every finger, and offered two triggers and two swiveling analog control pads. Neil understood why normal pilots might have a weird time adjusting to it, but it felt natural to him.

"On three, cadets," Jones's voice blared through Neil's headset. "One, two—"

On the major's "three," Neil excitedly pushed START, and his plane took off into the sky. He could feel his simulator's hydraulics working beneath him. On-screen, Trevor's plane was lit up as the man on fire, and Neil immediately shot to the left, to cover Trevor's blind spot as they raced forward. The first round passed in a blur. Biggs and Sam were eliminated early, both of them sacrificing their own planes to protect Trevor. The Jasons lasted longer, but soon they, too, had fallen in the enemy crossfire. Now it was just Trevor and Neil, dodging fire as they raced across the artificial landscape toward the goal line.

"Yes!" Neil exclaimed as he shot off another bogey just as they crossed the finish. He yanked off his headset and leaned back with a sigh of relief. He'd definitely won that round. Trevor would never have survived without him.

- -

"Round one to Grunsten," Jones's voice came over the speakers.

What? Neil thought angrily. How was that fair? He wanted to argue, but the next round was about to begin.

The second round was much harder than the first. The computer-generated enemies seemed more advanced. Every time Neil dodged, they were right there in front of him, as if they'd known what he was going to do before he even knew. Neil wasn't the only one to notice.

"They're figuring us out," Trevor's voice sounded in everyone's headset. "Okay. I'm gonna just go wild."

"What?" Neil demanded. "What do you mean?" But Trevor didn't answer.

Trevor began to fly dangerously and erratically, like he was closing his eyes and just turning the joystick around blindly. He created virtual havoc among the enemies, and for a split second Neil paused, admiring Trevor's plan in spite of himself. It was actually a good idea.

And then Neil saw, in the center of Trevor's storm of chaos, a direct shot at the enemy man on fire. It was only there for a split second, but that was all Neil needed. His instincts lightning-fast, he fired at the enemy—a perfect shot directly into the bogey's center. The round ended.

"Round two to Andertol," Jones announced. Neil smiled. He let his muscles relax for a brief second, cracking his knuckles as he stretched his arms.

"Nice job, Neil!" Samantha's voice resounded through Neil's headset.

"Okay, now final round, recruits," Jones said. Neil was tired—winded from the last round and his neck sore from the thrashing of the simulator—but he leaned forward in furious concentration, letting his mind block out everything except the game. He needed to win this.

As the level began, Neil noticed right away that this round had also been created with a significantly higher level of difficulty. The computer-generated enemies were faster than before, and there were many more of them.

"Let's stick together, Neil," Samantha suggested.

"Sure—I'll swing through that mountain range and flush them your way." Neil was so absorbed in the game that he didn't even realize he had just spoken to a girl.

Neil and Samantha worked well together, moving like a team and picking off fighters with practiced efficiency. When they had only a few enemies left, Neil spun away to take out Trevor—only to shoot down Biggs accidentally.

"Oh, sorry, man," Neil said, feeling terrible.

"*Namaste*, brother."

"*Gesundheit*," Neil replied.

Just as Neil circled back toward Samantha, a rocket hit her square in the nose, sending her fighter down in flames. It was only Neil and Trevor left now. Neil clamped down on the controls and made a hard left, hoping to get a lock on his final target.

"ManofAshley, thought you should know you have lost to B4rrelR0ll. Oh, and you should really be more careful of your blind spots," said Trevor, who appeared from high above Neil on the right and then barreled down rapidly. Two rockets hit Neil at once, and his screen faded to black.

The simulator doors opened with a hiss, and the six pilots crawled out. Neil stumbled forward, still in shock from the abrupt end to the game. He should have seen that coming. And he should have guessed that Trevor was none other than B4rrelR0ll.

Jones was waiting outside the simulation chamber, seemingly pleased. He stood with the other recruits, fresh off the Decider, and started to brief them for the simulation chambers. Neil stepped out into the hall, and Samantha followed.

"We almost had that one," she said, leaning against the wall. "Reminded me of that huge team game we had a few weeks ago, yeah?"

Neil froze. Samantha was still talking, but Neil didn't hear her. An otherworldly buzz was raging through his ears.

Of course, Neil thought. *Samantha* was ShooterSam. The guy he shared his embarrassing stories with, who made him laugh, who knew him better than anyone else in the world. His *best friend*.

Except, it turned out, *he* was a *she*.

CHAPTER 7

NEIL MUMBLED SOMETHING UNINTELLIGIBLE TO SAM AND hurried down the hall to the bathroom. He needed a minute alone to process this. He pushed through the doorway, only to run directly into Biggs.

"Hey, man, slow down," Biggs said, following Neil back into the bathroom. "What's wrong? You just kicked some major butt on the sim. Almost took that last one."

"Dude, I'm in trouble," Neil said, locking himself into a stall.

"How bad? I can get you to Mexico by horseback within a day, tops. I know people."

"What? No, man, not that kind of trouble."

"Oh, gotcha. All right, what's up for real, then?"

"It's Samantha. *Sam*," Neil said, unlocking the door and facing Biggs.

"Ooh! You interested?"

Neil felt himself blush. "No, it's not that at all. She's *ShooterSam*."

"Yeah, man, you guys play together, like, all the time. Gotta be cool to finally meet."

"That's the thing. I—I thought . . . well, I thought that *she* was a *he*," Neil stammered, turning on a faucet.

"You didn't know that she was a *she*?" Biggs asked, confused.

"No!" Neil shouted, and closed his eyes. He thought back to all their conversations. Whenever they'd talked about school, or family, or friends, Neil had always just assumed that the stories he heard were being told by a guy. "I don't know; it just never got mentioned!" Neil said finally. "I mean, we would pause games to both run to the bathroom, but I just always assumed we were both standing up."

- -

Biggs pondered this for a second, catching Neil's glance in a mirror.

Neil sighed and reached for a paper towel. "I just . . . I'm not really good at talking to girls. The only ones I talk to are the ones I'm related to by blood, and even then I'm not entirely sure about my sister, Janey. I think she's half ninja."

"Dude, chill. You just need to use some of my Biggs charm," Biggs said, pulling open the door to the hallway.

"But I don't have any Biggs ch—" Neil began to say, until he spotted Sam leaning against the wall, her legs making a 4.

"Hey, guys, Major Jones asked me to come find you," Sam said, walking toward Neil and Biggs. "We're ready to be 'decisioned,' or whatever."

"Well, you found us!" Neil said, a bit too enthusiastically. He could feel himself beginning to sweat. Biggs glanced his way with a knowing look that only sort of calmed him down.

"*Right on*, I think, is what my excited friend is trying to say," Biggs added.

"Oookay," said Sam, smiling a little. "Now, let's pull chocks, boys. We gotta be there in two minutes."

"How do you know all these military terms?" Biggs asked as he and Neil started after Sam. "I'm just getting the hang of military time. Like, do you say *oh* before every time? Or just sometimes? Can I pepper it in occasionally at the end?"

"You'll get the hang of it," Sam replied. "My dad's Army, so I've just always been around it."

"Cool," replied Biggs. "I'm the same way. My dad lived in a giant fir tree for a year, so I know what you mean."

Sam blinked at Biggs in confusion, then shook her head as if giving up on trying to understand. She paused for a moment in the hallway, undid her pigtails, flipped her hair forward, and pulled it back into a high ponytail. Her hair smelled faintly of coconut. Neil could see that her ears weren't pierced.

"Neil, you pick up any good terms from your folks?" Sam asked, oblivious to the fact that Neil was staring. "You said one time your dad was a scientist?"

"Oh, uh, well," Neil stammered. His father was a scientist of sorts. Since this usually ended up with laughs from the likes of Tommy Scott, he rarely mentioned it.

"Yeah, I mean he's got scientist *tendencies*, maybe?"

Neil said. "Or something. He works with paleontologists and archaeologists. It's boring, I know—"

"Boring? No way! I love dinosaurs. They're one of my top seventeen favorite things!" Sam beamed. "Does he work with the exhuming? Or on-site?"

"Um . . ." The problem was, Neil actually had no idea what his dad did all day. Every time he asked, his dad just laughed and gave him dinosaur stickers. Neil had given up on figuring it out. "I know that he has meetings, makes calls, wears a tie on Mondays . . . oh, and sometimes he comes home with ice cream?" Neil was never one to talk business, especially once cookies and/or ice cream were made available.

"Well, I'm sure it's really cool. Has he helped discover any new species?" Sam asked, her interest increasing proportionally to Neil's armpit sweat.

"I heard he just made a big find. The ecksbocksosaurus," Biggs interrupted.

Sam tilted her head. "Oh, wow. That must have just happened. I've never even heard of it. Is it an ankylosaur?"

"Something like that." Neil shrugged, giving Biggs a glare. If this was the Biggs charm, Neil wasn't sure if he needed much more of it.

"Well, either way, that's cool," Sam said, plunging her hand into her pocket. She pulled out an oblong, flat rock, which fit perfectly in the smooth palm of her hand. Neil noticed she wore a bracelet of a thin, braided rope and had the faint remnants of purple nail polish still clinging to the centers of her nails.

"This is my good luck charm. It's a trilobite," she said, opening her fingers to display the fossilized remnants of a creature that lived millions of years ago.

As she held it out for Neil to see, Trevor appeared from around the corner, with Jason 1 and Jason 2 on either side.

"I'll take that," Trevor said, trying to grab the artifact, but Sam's hand retracted quickly, like a Venus flytrap.

"In your dreams," Sam snapped, stowing one-seventeenth of her passions away from eyesight.

Trevor mimicked a response and then fell in line as Neil, Sam, and Biggs turned to head down the hallway to the Decider. Neil glanced back at the two boys trailing behind with Trevor. For having the same name, they couldn't have looked more different. Jason 1 was African American, with short buzzed hair. He was only an inch shorter than Biggs, the tallest recruit, and moved with an athletic energy. Jason 2, on the other hand, had a huge, almond-shaped head, with oversize round ears and a small ski ramp of a nose. Moles dotted his pale skin, like Cocoa Puffs in a sea of skim milk. He was quiet and always seemed to have his hands shoved down into his pants pockets.

"Hey, Ashley, if you're lucky, maybe I'll teach you to actually fly one of those fighters someday," Trevor challenged as he caught Neil's stare.

"Yeah? Well, you're lucky that the sim training was only three rounds, because Neil would have destroyed you in the next one," Sam retorted.

"Ooh, Ashley's new girlfriend gonna do the talking for him?" Trevor laughed.

"I knew from the way he flies that that kid would be a jerk," Sam said under her breath, rolling her eyes.

Neil said nothing. He couldn't think about anything except what was up ahead, the mysterious challenge that would determine his fate. The Decider.

CHAPTER

8

"THIS WAY, RECRUITS," LOPEZ SAID, WAVING THEM THROUGH an open door that could only lead to the Decider. Everyone gulped and then, one by one, filed inside.

The first thing that struck Neil was the bright light. Early-morning sunlight shone through a glass ceiling onto an open, expansive facility. Neil could see the edges of mountains outside the glass, the base securely nestled in a mountain range.

Directly below the glass dome, and taking up the entire room, was a mammoth, snaking obstacle course.

By Neil's count, it boasted seven different challenges, starting with dangling tires to crawl through and then segueing into a series of horizontal wooden rails to hop over and crawl under. Next were cargo nets, monkey bars, and swinging ropes, all over a pit of drab brownish water and a springy rectangular trampoline for them to jump across a deep, muddy trench. That led up to a ten-foot-tall wooden climbing wall. At the top was a platform where a cowbell hung suspended from a fraying rope. As Neil studied the course, an air horn blasted, shaking his concentration and his nerves.

"Recruits, welcome to the Decider." Jones waved an arm at the array of equipment before them.

"In order to fly with the Air Force, every recruit has to finish the course in under seventy-five seconds. But since you may not all have the, ah, *physical skills*, let's just say a completion of the course will suffice."

Neil rubbed his biceps, or at least the areas of his arms where biceps were meant to be. *I've got physical skills*, he thought. *Like opening bags of chips. Or tricky pickle jars.*

"Wells and Lopez will show you all how it's done. To this day, they hold the two fastest times, separated by only a half second."

The two soldiers calmly bumped their fists together, clearly proud of their records. Neil winced at the thought of how hard their knuckles must be.

"Our first-place finisher is guaranteed a seat on the Chameleon for the mission," Jones announced.

I'm getting in that jet fighter, Neil thought furiously.

"Oh, and you also get this," he added, holding up a platinum-colored cowbell trophy, a sparkling replica of the one signaling the noisy finish line of the obstacle course. "'The Decision Maker.' Standard reward for the fastest new recruit."

Neil's eyes lit up, and he wondered how much space it would take up on his living-room mantel. It was as big as at least eight or nine of Janey's karate awards put together.

Jones turned to his men. "Wells, Lopez, let's show them how it's done."

At the sound of another horn, the two attacked the course. They gracefully slithered through the dangling tires, hopped over and went under the wooden planks with ease, and traversed the murky water with calculated swoops of their arms. In just one step, they jumped the trench and grabbed the top of the wall with only one arm each, hoisting themselves up in a single motion. Then, together, they rattled the metal bell with force as Jones punched the stopwatch in his hand. He looked like a proud father. Neil felt light-headed just seeing it all happen.

"Not your best, gentlemen. But still impressive. Now, recruits, it's your turn. I need to see hustle. Please don't take longer than ten minutes. Otherwise I'm retiring."

The six kids began shaking their wrists to loosen up, some pulling their arms across their bodies in an attempt to stretch. But then, without warning, the sound of the starting horn filled the room again.

"*Go!*" Jones yelled, his voice hoarse.

The crew dived headfirst for the tires, most of them whining as their faces scraped against the rigid, unforgiving rubber. Neil was skinny, though, and managed to snake his way through. *Pretend it's a video game*, he told himself as he slithered through the last tire and stumbled forward. *Just keep going.*

Neil risked a quick glance back and saw that Jason 2 was right behind him, stuck diagonally in the tires and squirming in frustration. Neil grabbed Jason's outstretched hand and gave a quick tug. As Jason's legs pulled free, Neil noticed a full-body spandex bodysuit underneath his uniform. It was green, sparkly, and skin-tight, like a superhero costume of some kind.

"Thanks," Jason 2 gasped as he wobbled out.

"Is that a costu—" Neil started to ask, but Jason 2 cut him off.

"Shh!" He placed a long, bony finger to his lips and then took off ahead, leaving Neil in his wake. Neil looked up to see Jason 1 waving him on.

Neil frowned in concentration and started on the boards. He rolled under the first and then jumped over the next, continuing as the boards slowly grew lower and higher in comparison to the ground.

The recruits stuck together as they made their way through the course, helping one another through the toughest parts, and eventually, they all gathered before the murky water, catching their breath and studying what lay before them.

"Cannonballlll!" Jason 2 suddenly yelled, and took a running jump into the gross-looking water, splashing all over Trevor. *That's one way of doing it*, Neil thought with a smile as he hopped onto the monkey bars above the water. With Sam, Trevor, and Biggs at either side,

Neil moved forward slowly, the skin from his hands peeling against the rough metal of the bars, his bony knees knocking together like human wind chimes.

Finally, they all stood in front of the giant trampoline that they needed to jump on to cross the muddy ditch below. "Me first!" Jason 1 shouted, launching himself off the trampoline. But his jump was too short, and he landed headfirst in the deep pit of mud. Laughing, Trevor started up next, only to fall like a flailing sack of potatoes and land next to Jason 1.

One by one, the rest of the recruits all tried to jump across, but no one seemed to have enough leg strength for a big-enough leap. "Come on, recruits!" Jones was yelling, his face red. But after Biggs failed miserably at a Fosbury Flop approach, Neil found himself the only recruit left standing on unmuddy ground.

This is your chance, Neil told himself. *You make this and you're in that plane. Maybe even a pilot.*

Neil bounced up and down on his tiptoes, then took a running start. He pushed off the trampoline with all his might, his legs extending behind him as he flew like a gazelle over the trench full of mud-soaked gamers, their alligator arms snapping under his frame. Neil landed on the opposite side, his left leg dangling into the trench. Panting from excitement and sheer disbelief, he quickly pulled himself up to examine the final obstacle: a giant, flat climbing wall. There were no handholds or footholds, and there was no way he was tall enough just to leap and pull himself onto the top platform like Wells and Lopez had done. But there was nothing else to do. Neil's eyes fixed on the bell positioned above, and he summoned all the energy he had left in his body. With a grunt, he jumped as high as he could. Within a foot of the top, his hands scrambled for something to grab onto, and finding nothing, he slid back down, landing in a tangle of wiry limbs.

"Neil. You can't get up there alone. If you toss us that rope and let us all up, we can all help lift you to the top of the wall," called Trevor from the deep, sticky pit.

"Yeah, right," said Neil, turning back to face the wall. He knew better than to trust Trevor.

"Ignore Trevor," Sam called out as if reading his mind. "Just let me have the rope. I'll help."

"No mercy, recruits! Clock is ticking!" Jones hollered from the sideline.

Neil's lungs burned, and while holding his hands

above his head for staccato gasps, he caught Jones's eye, which was gleaming with a crazed kind of excitement. Neil wondered if holidays at the Jones household involved some sort of festive obstacle course.

Deep down, Neil knew that Sam was right. Still catching his breath, he grabbed the length of rope attached to the base of the wall and tossed its free end into the pit, twirling it to within Sam's reach.

Sam climbed out first, followed by Trevor and the others all muddy and soaked, like swamp hatchlings that had lost their tails. Jason 2 was the last to crawl out, and Neil reached down to give him a hand. As he pulled Jason 2 up over the edge, Jason's shirt lifted at the hem, revealing more of the jumpsuit that he was wearing underneath. Neil could see a white belt around Jason's spandex-clad midsection.

"I have to ask," Neil said. "What's your superhero name?"

"The Shrieking Salamander," Jason 2 whispered as he and Neil hurried back to the wall, where the others were all gathered. "My powers are legendary."

"Got it," Neil confirmed as he turned to watch Trevor trying to scramble to the top of the wall first. The rest of the group were jumping up and flinging their bodies at the wall, each of their jumps leaving muddy outlines of their bodies that seemed to get lower and lower as they steadily lost energy.

"Neil," Sam offered, "how about me and Biggs give you a boost? We would still be stuck in that ditch if it wasn't for you."

"Totally. I wanna see you win this thing," said Biggs, who had twisted his ankle in the fall and couldn't leap. "If nothing else as a tribute to the good sideburn hair you lost this morning."

Neil took an instinctive step backward as Biggs and Sam clasped their hands, creating a step. Experience had taught him that anyone creating a bridge with their hands was preparing just to chuck him as far as they could, like a human cannonball. But then he looked into their eyes and reminded himself that Biggs and Sam were his friends. New friends. *Well, new old friends, sort of.*

"Okay," he said, and put a confident boot on their hands. They hoisted him as high as they could. "Almost there . . . ," Neil grunted, his fingertips just touching the top of the platform.

"Now try," Biggs said, lifting Neil up a few extra

inches. It was just enough for Neil to grab a firm hold of the platform. His stomach fluttered with excitement. He was moments away from getting a guaranteed spot on that plane.

But just as Neil started to lift his skinny frame to the top, he felt the hands of someone crawling up his back.

"Hey!" Neil yelled. He looked back to see Trevor stepping on Biggs's face and then jabbing his knee right into Neil's shoulder. Using Neil as a human ladder, Trevor clambered over him and then up onto the platform, clanging the cowbell loudly in victory, smirking at Neil. Neil felt like he was going to throw up.

★   ★   ★

Neil and the others reported back to their bunks, quickly throwing their new military clothes into canvas backpacks. They were to bring their uniforms to the briefing session, after which they would either depart for the mission or head out on the first commercial flight home. A nervous, excited energy found its way into every conversation.

As he hurried between bunks, Neil bumped shoulders with one of the kids from the other training group, knocking the neat pile of clothes out of his hands and onto the floor.

"Oh, sorry," Neil said, kneeling to help pick up the kid's stuff. The boy had short, spiky black hair that seemed capable of stabbing cheese cubes. Neil handed him a pair of camouflage pants that had fallen. "Here ya go. I'm Neil, by the way."

"Thanks. I'm Jo-yung, but most everybody calls me JP. Nice to meet you. I think we both played in that giant multiplayer game last weekend, if I'm not mistaken." He shoved the rest of his clothes into his bag. Clear braces were stuck to his teeth, giving him a slight lisp. "I'm jp4343."

"Oh wait, are you the guy who fell asleep and flew into that bridge right at the end?" Neil asked.

"Ha, yes, that was me. I was in Taiwan for a week visiting family. There's a fifteen-hour time difference, so after a while I totally crashed. In the game, and on my grandparents' basement couch." He smiled nervously.

"Nice," Neil said. "You were really good, though, crash or no crash."

"Thanks. And sorry for any snoring!" JP laughed. "It's cool—if you think about it, I was sort of playing from the future."

"Did you say you're from the future?" Biggs

interrupted from his bed. "Do you know if we ever figure out space travel? Or if we've mastered sustainable vegetarian beef jerky? What are the next winning lottery numbers?" Strands of hair fell in front of Biggs's face as he wrestled to zip his backpack closed. It was stuffed so full, Neil wondered where Biggs had even gotten all that stuff. They had all been issued the same set of gear. "I'm Biggs, by the by," Biggs said, blowing the hair out of his eyes.

JP looked more than a bit confused as he introduced himself. Neil was beginning to understand that this was something of a typical reaction to people meeting Biggs for the first time.

"Anyway, I think I'm going to head out. It doesn't seem that the major tolerates tardiness," said JP.

"See you in there!" yelled Biggs a little too loudly from under the bed. Biggs apparently possessed a special kind of messiness that made it seem like he had been on the base for weeks, when it had been only one night. He crawled through his bunk bed searching for dirty socks and shirts like he was on some kind of smelly Easter egg hunt.

"Actually, I'm all good to go, too," said Neil. "Maybe

I'll just meet you there. Okay?"

Biggs poked his head out from under his bed. "All good, brother. Just took a quick underwear roll call, and we're down only one. Also, gettin' some pretty intense smells down here, too. You go ahead."

Neil grabbed his pack and walked with JP. Two other recruits held the door open, and Neil noticed that they looked exactly the same, something he hadn't realized earlier. They were both the same height, very energetic, and sported the same thick, wavy brown hair.

"Monozygote?" asked JP as they all walked together.

"Huh?" Neil asked. The other two guys seemed equally confused.

"Oh, sorry. That's the scientific term for identical twins. You are, right?" said JP.

"Yes," one of the brothers replied, just as the other said, "Sort of." They spoke with a hint of country twang and were each missing a front tooth, one on the right and the other on the left.

"I mean, we *are* twins," the brother with the missing right front tooth piped in. "I'm three minutes older, though. And technically, I guess, we're identical. But anyone who knows us can tell us apart. Name's Dale," the boy said, holding up his dog tags as proof.

"Neil," Neil said, offering his hand. The boy shook it, grasping both sides in a friendly way. The hair just above his forehead arched wildly before blending into something more manageable. Neil remembered that the term was "cowlick," and for the first time, he thought the word made sense. Dale's hair definitely had that "freshly licked by a farm animal" swirl. "JP and I were just talking about how we were in that multiplayer game last week." he said. "What are your user names? I'm ManofNeil."

"You're ManofNeil?" Dale exclaimed. "You're, like, a gaming *ninja*! Did you hear that? This is ManofNeil!" Dale said, turning to his brother and poking Neil in the arm.

"No way!" said his twin.

"We've always wanted to play with you," Dale continued, "but we only play Chameleon on Sundays for the big team game."

"Ah, I'm a Saturday guy myself," said Neil, blushing from the attention. "But I'll have to play with you sometime, Dale and . . ."

"Waffles," the other brother squeaked.

"Oh, um, I think we could maybe head back to the

mess hall if you're hungry," Neil responded to the odd remark. "I was thinking about slipping a couple bagels in my pockets, too."

"No, the name's Waffles. Not legally, but everybody calls me Waffles." He seemed full of energy, his elastic limbs always moving in a subtly sporadic sway. Neil recognized a bit of himself in Waffles's actions—that feeling of always wanting to be tinkering or controlling something.

"Cool," JP said, not flinching at the craziness of the nickname as more introductions were made all around.

They reached the door to the meeting room, where Jones was waiting to announce the results of the training, and they all fell silent. Neil's stomach began to clench as he watched the major pace in front of a podium. This was it.

As they took their seats, Neil noticed something else. In the front row sat a new recruit, a girl whom Neil hadn't seen before. She was on the shorter side, with dark-caramel-colored skin and scraggly hair that made it look like she'd been electrocuted.

"Recruits, take your seats," ordered Jones while the last few stragglers filed in. "For those of you who haven't yet met her, this is Corinne Adams, our twelfth recruit selected to train for the mission." Corinne blinked her eyes quickly, shifting from side to side.

"You might remember the young man who requested to leave last night," the major said, his voice sheepish. "Corinne here is taking his place. Or rather, taking her *original* place. Corin Adams instead of Corinne Adams." Jones paused to glare at a trembling soldier behind a laptop to his left. "I've been assured that a clerical error of this nature won't happen again.

"And now, what you've all been waiting for . . ." A still, serious quiet fell over the room. Neil took a deep breath. It felt as if everything in his life, all the hundreds of hours of gaming, had led him to this single moment. He wanted to be selected so badly that his bones ached. Then again, that could also be because he had spit out the vitamins his mom had tried to force-feed him from ages five to seven.

"Let me say first that there's been a change of plans," Jones continued, looking somber.

A groan rippled through the room.

"What do you mean? You're not taking anybody?" Trevor growled. "You promised we'd have a chance!"

"Easy there, Grunsten. I didn't say that," Jones

reassured him. "Actually, it's the opposite."

Neil was intrigued. *Opposite?*

"Next to all our trained pilots who attempted the sim-ulator, you twelve had the best scores—by nearly double. And these are Navy and Air Force pilots with thousands of hours of logged flying," Jones said. "Needless to say, we were impressed. And to be frank, surprised."

"Excuse me, Frank?" asked Biggs, raising his hand. "Does this mean—" But Jones cut him off.

"So instead of just taking one Chameleon, we'll be taking the three that we have. This mission is going to be more intense than we anticipated and we could use the extra manpower. My right- and left-hand men here will be joining us," he said, pointing to Wells and Lopez.

"You'll receive the full mission briefing in one hour, but for now, I'd like to announce the three of you who will be flying as lead pilots on the mission.

"First, Trevor Grunsten, who tied for the best score in the simulation as well as winning his heat on the Decider."

Neil rolled his eyes as Trevor stood up, applauding himself loudly.

- -

"Jo-yung Phe." JP nodded in acknowledgment. "And finally . . ."

Neil leaned forward, anxious to hear his name.

"Corinne Adams."

Neil felt the blood rush down to his knees. He wouldn't be piloting one of the Chameleons after all. He dropped his head, doing his best to hide his disappointment.

"I'll announce copilots and auxiliary seats after the briefing. See you in an hour, recruits," the major concluded. He paused, as if weighing his next words, then sighed heavily.

"Welcome to the Air Force, kids. We're counting on you."

CHAPTER

9

AN HOUR LATER, NEIL STEPPED INTO THE HANGAR NOW abuzz with preflight preparations. Cables for fuel and diagnostics snaked their way across the concrete floor to three sleek fighter jets. The giant room echoed with noise as orders were clarified and lists were double-checked.

Three flight technicians were working double time to have the jets ready for takeoff within the hour. Neil and his new friends did their best to skirt the frantic engineers, not wanting to get in the way of any vital preparation. Neil was fascinated by the speed and precision with which they handled such important machinery. Since everything was so top secret, only these three mechanics knew what needed to be done, and none of them wasted a single movement. The sounds of hydraulic pumps, like the tools used in race-car pits, rang out from all directions.

Neil didn't want to peel his eyes away for one minute, but he snapped to attention when he heard Jones's gruff voice behind him. He watched the major wait to address his new recruits, his lower right lip bulging with sunflower seeds. Jones was wearing the same camouflage flight jumpsuit as the recruits, but while they looked scrawny, the major seemed somehow bigger than Neil remembered.

"Well, this looks like everyone," Jones remarked as he glanced past Neil. Neil pivoted around to see Biggs and the remaining recruits scurrying into the cavernous metal hangar.

Jones brought his thumb and forefinger up to his mouth and whistled, loudly. It was the kind of up, then down, and back up again whistle that Neil had heard fathers do at Janey's karate tournaments.

Neil thought back to a few months ago, when he'd stared into a mirror for fifty-seven straight minutes in an attempt to re-create such a whistle. His only success had been to produce an alarming amount of slobber.

"Okay, recruits, this is it," Jones began. "In addition to the lead pilots and the copilots, who I will announce momentarily, there will be two more of you flying in each Chameleon as auxiliary, *err*, backup pilots. Listen up for your name." He took out his list. "Andertol"—Neil was surprised to hear his own name called first—"you'll be copilot supporting . . . Grunsten."

You've got to be kidding me, Neil thought as he turned his head away from the weaselly smile spreading across Trevor's face. It almost wasn't worth being a copilot if he had to fly with Trevor. Sam patted him on the shoulder, and he took a deep breath.

As Jones went on reading the list of the rest of the copilots, and the auxiliaries who would be helping with the invisibility and radar technology, Neil brightened up when he heard he'd be flying with Biggs. Maybe it wouldn't be *so* bad. He wanted to whisper a joke, but he worried that Jones might hear. And he doubted Jones would think it was funny.

"Okay, everybody," Jones said, folding the list and placing it in his pocket. "Know which plane you're in?

Good. I'll keep this short and sweet. This is a simple recovery mission for a missing Chameleon fighter and the two soldiers flying it."

Neil kept an eye on the sunflower seeds still curled away in Jones's lip. So far, he hadn't seen him spit out any shells. He wondered if Jones was swallowing them, and if they had some kind of years-long digestion process, like chewing gum.

"From here on out, the three of us are in charge," Jones barked, gesturing to Lopez and Wells. "While these things normally only fit four, we'll be riding in the emergency jump seat. We wanted to bring an extra recruit in each craft to serve as pilot for the return if our soldiers are unable to operate the missing fighter. Once the missing Chameleon is recovered, we'll have one of the copilots on standby to fly it home, if necessary."

Neil knew right away that he wanted to be that pilot.

"You will each report to your assigned soldier, and they will both report to me. Now, before we set out for the missing plane, we will be making a stop at the USS *Martin Van Buren*. It's an aircraft carrier in the Pacific about ninety clicks west and a few more south," Jones continued. "That will give you a chance to get a feel for the aircraft, and maybe even let our copilots take a spin at it. From there, our mission starts.

"Corinne, your team is with Lopez. JP, you're with Wells. Grunsten, you're with me. That means you're flying lead in formation."

"Sir, yes, sir!" Trevor said with an excited nod. Neil felt his heart start beating at double speed. He was flying in the lead plane—which might just mean he had the best chance of piloting the missing plane once they'd found it.

"Now, cadets, I want to make one thing clear. While you all learned these skills from a game . . . *this*," Jones said, pointing to the nearest Chameleon, "*this* is *not* a game. There are no more restarts. Game over means *game over*. But if you're like me, that's the way you like it. So, you ready?"

"Sir, yes, sir!" everyone yelled, somewhat together this time.

Neil grabbed his in-flight jumpsuit out of a pile and pulled it over his regulation canvas pants and plain gray shirt. It was like an ill-fitting beige cocoon—but a very official-looking one. Tying his shoes, Neil looked up at the metal staircase firmly planted in front of the jet he'd be copiloting. It was a long way up.

All at once, the cockpit on each jet slid open, and Neil and the others warily climbed up into their fighters.

The interior looked exactly as it did in Chameleon. Unlike in standard military jets, the cockpit seated the pilots next to each other rather than in front of each other. A console of controls was situated between the pilot and the copilot, and the seats were facing a sprawling dashboard of HD displays and various buttons. The backs of the seats were pressed to the backs of those for the two auxiliary pilots, causing them to face in the other direction out the rear of the jet.

Neil shimmied past Trevor's pilot seat and sank into his own. He put his hands up as the flight technician fastened him into his seat, firmly securing a safety harness that covered both shoulders. A helmet with a sliding shaded visor was handed to him, with a mouthpiece to be snapped on during flight for communication and oxygen flow.

"So how's this invisibility stuff work, anyway?" Neil asked.

"Scales," said the flight technician. He wore a jumpsuit similar to Neil's, a pencil haphazardly shoved into his thick, springy hair.

"Scales?" Neil asked.

"Like a chameleon. An actual chameleon," replied the soldier, making sure Neil's in-flight mask was working properly. Seeing Neil's confusion, he went on. "In nature, chameleons have scales made up of chromatophores, things that kind of store colors in little vesicles. These change color when signaled to do so. Our invisibility works the same way. There are millions of microscopic scales that cover the aircraft, and they all help bend the light hitting the entirety of the plane, even on the glass of the cockpit. From any angle, you can see only a perfect re-creation of the ship's outer environment."

"Whoa, cool," Neil said.

"Future is now, kid." In his grip, the flight technician held a shiny white tablet. He whisked through pages of electronic information until he found the one he was after.

"If you could, press your hand here," he said, tilting the cool glass rectangle toward Neil. Neil touched the screen and watched as a line scrolled from top to bottom, tracing every detail of his hand.

"Now whenever you need to get in, just place your hand on any part of the craft. The cockpit will slide right open, even if it's invisible," the soldier explained. "This works for any of the Chameleons. Once you're in the system, any of them will open for you."

He patted Neil on the top of his helmet and the side of the fighter twice before he disappeared out of sight. Neil secured his helmet and radioed to Sam.

"ManofNeil to ShooterSam . . . Samantha. Miss Shooter Samantha," Neil fumbled.

"Neil, it's just me, Sam."

As Neil searched for something to say to Sam, Trevor labored into his seat, his eyes focusing on the controls in front of him.

"What's up, compadres?" chirped Biggs, who was stepping on board. He slapped Neil and Trevor on the back and settled into his seat behind Trevor. "This thing got cup holders?"

"My lords," said Riley, following Biggs onto the plane.

As Biggs and the others proceeded with safety checks and the palm scan, Jones walked up the stairs and poked his head into the doorway of the aircraft. In the cramped space, he moved with the finesse and grace of a recently injured rhinoceros.

"Recruits," he grunted.

"We look forward to soaring in this iron-forged, bird-less carriage with you, Our Jones," said Riley. Jones craned his neck and cupped his hand around his right ear.

"What was that? You all should speak toward my left side. Have a bit of trouble hearing outta this ear," Jones explained.

"'Tis nothing of import," Riley said sheepishly.

★ ★ ★

Trevor, Neil, Riley, and Biggs all watched as Jones struggled to squeeze into his emergency jump seat at the back of the plane. Neil felt suddenly grateful that he wasn't in Biggs's or Riley's seat. They would have to spend the entire flight looking directly at Jones.

"Okay," Jones said into his radio mouthpiece after the cockpit door was sealed shut. "Let's fly."

Neil couldn't have agreed more.

As the towering metal doors of the hangars clanked open, the three fighter jets rolled out onto the runway. Neil's eyes followed the painted directional lines on the runway below. Soldiers directed traffic with illuminated orange wands, their arms rhythmically turning like human windmills.

Chameleons were designed not to need a long runway for a smooth takeoff. The directional thrusters below the cockpit let the fighters hover almost straight up, allowing for quick and nearly silent ascents and descents. Even though Neil knew they didn't need the room, he still felt his stomach twisting in knots as they approached the beginning of the tarmac.

"This is Chameleon Alpha, requesting permission for takeoff," Jones said over his communication system.

"You are cleared for takeoff, Alpha team," replied a voice from the flight deck.

Without needing any more encouragement, Trevor fired the thrusters below, and the jet rose with a surge into the air. They had liftoff.

CHAPTER

10

THE JET TORE THROUGH THE CLOUDS AS IF THEY WERE THE computer-simulated clouds Neil was used to facing, leaving only a blue frontier in all directions.

As Neil eyed his jet's rapidly rising altimeter, the blood in his temples pounded and he thought back to a night, months earlier, when he'd suddenly grown frustrated with online gaming. He'd stayed up into the wee hours of the morning researching the actual experience of flight so he could know what it felt like to pilot a real fighter jet. That night, Neil spent hours watching online videos, studying flight maps, and reading blog posts of former pilots. The next day, he'd gone back to gaming, feeling more like an actual pilot, having a better idea of the reality of the game he was playing.

How wrong he'd been. Nothing, none of those videos or blog entries, really prepared him for how cool the real thing felt. It was better than he could have ever imagined.

Suddenly, the jet fighter shot up at a steeper angle than Neil thought possible.

"Whoa." Neil held on to the controls in front of him, his stomach dropping to his knees. *Maybe having a barf bag around would have been a good idea.*

"Increase the thrust, copilot," instructed Trevor. "We'll climb up in altitude and look to roll right."

"I know," Neil said, catching his breath. Neil wasn't thrilled to be taking orders from Trevor, but he felt like he had no choice. He grabbed the grooved metallic control in the thin console between the pilots.

Their jet leveled while capping hundreds of miles per hour, and Neil was surprised to feel nearly motionless. And yet he sensed, too, that the plane could go faster still. It was being held back, like a boat engine stuck in seaweed, its propellers lurching to break free. It was time to put the pedal to the metal. Or a joystick to the sky.

"Recruits," Jones said over the radio to everyone, "I want to run through terms quickly, just so you're familiar. To fly up, it's—"

"Pitch. We know," Trevor said.

"And yaw. What I mean by yaw is—"

"Left, right," said the duo of Dale and Waffles over the radio.

"Side to side," added JP.

"We have the internet. You'd be shocked at how much we know," said Neil. The group laughed.

"Well, can the internet teach you what the battlefield really looks like? How it feels to fly a jet engine? Or break the sound barrier? The smell of freedom from a hard-fought victory?"

"Wait, you've got that scent? Are you sandbaggin' me on that smell, Mr. Jones?" Biggs barged in.

"Hurbigg, it's Major Jones. Were you raised by wolves or something?"

"It was only a week, and I'd rather not talk about it."

Meanwhile, Trevor straightened his back and tightened his grip on the controls.

"So you don't think we can fly, Jonesy? Copilot, ready the afterburners," Trevor said.

Trevor kept the fighter aimed forward but suddenly had Neil throttle back.

"What are you doing?" Neil asked as he eased on the speed of their craft. In the same motion, Trevor rolled right and aimed the nose of the plane down. The fighter dived toward the brown rocky landscape dead ahead.

From hours of virtual piloting, Neil now realized Trevor was trying a split S. It was tricky—the plane dived down and turned, then turned again to accelerate in another direction. When the move was performed correctly, the plane made a swooping S shape, exiting the maneuver going either directly left, right, or opposite from where it started.

"Grunsten, watch your—" Jones began, but stopped as the g-force suddenly pushed down on everyone. Neil felt as if a huge person, a sumo wrestler maybe, was sitting right on top of him. But even as he gritted his teeth at the feeling of being smushed, he couldn't help noticing how flawless and precise Trevor was. As the plane moved smoothly out of the roll, Neil punched the throttle.

"Woo!" Trevor yelled, and even Neil joined in.

"That was awesome," Neil agreed, unleashing the afterburners as their craft rocketed forward, like being fired from a slingshot.

"In my three decades of service, I've never seen a pilot do that without hundreds or thousands of flight hours logged," an impressed Jones said over his headset. "I'd be furious if you hadn't done it perfectly." Trevor smiled. "But let's hand the controls over to copilots, quickly. They need to get a feel for the planes, too, just in case."

Trevor's smirk faded as his hands reluctantly moved from the controls to the throttle.

Neil confidently reached for the joystick in front of his seat. It felt like second nature, like riding a bike after a long winter spent indoors. *Except this bike doesn't have giant orange safety flags attached to the back.* Neil's mother was aggressive about bike safety.

"You need to try to *feel* your aircraft," Jones encouraged. "You need to become a part of it."

This stuck with Neil. As he effortlessly cut through the air, he felt as if the fighter jet was an extension of himself, as if he simply had to think what he wanted it to do and then it would happen.

On the interactive visors on everyone's helmets, co-ordinates of the aircraft carrier began to flash in vivid detail. The distance to the carrier was calculated and shown beneath. The Chameleons had sped past the coastline and were now out over the churning currents of endless sea.

"Copilots, we'll be approaching our first destination, the USS *Martin Van Buren*," said Jones. A three-dimensional satellite image of a massive aircraft carrier came into the center of each display. Planes and complicated weaponry dotted the floating runway. It turned slowly, tiny soldiers moving around on its deck.

"What's on all their faces?" asked Biggs. Neil toggled the controls on the joystick in front of him to zoom in. He saw what Biggs was talking about. On either side of the soldiers' faces, it looked as if some kind of furry wildlife had recently died there.

"Oh, the chops." Jones groaned, as if the question came up frequently. "Well, as per military rules, soldiers aren't allowed facial hair. But there's the name loophole."

"The name loophole?" Neil asked.

"Basically, a rule was grandfathered in that the only style of facial hair a soldier can have is that of the ship's namesake. So, for example, the crew on the USS *Lincoln* gets beards," Jones explained. An electronic bust of Van Buren appeared on the visor displays. "Unfortunately, President Van Buren enjoyed what we in the business like to call muttonchops. Those big patches of sideburn hair that tend to grow more out than down. Sadly, it seems the men of the ship are keeping that disgusting tradition alive." Jones cleared his throat. "But you'll see all that soon enough. Coordinates set?"

Neil and the others now piloting—Sam on his left and Yuri on his right—replied with an affirmative, and Jones gave them the go-ahead to start flying out of formation.

"Hey, Biggs and Riley, how you guys doing back there?" Neil asked.

"Great, man. This video camouflage stuff is awesome," Biggs said. "I think I can get it to play giant cat videos. For later."

"And I'm ready if you need me, your lordship," piped up Riley.

Neil made a mental note to do a quick Google search

on his phone for Renaissance terms once they were safely on the ground. He turned his attention back to the monitor, where the GPS beacon for the aircraft carrier was quickly approaching, and began to prepare for landing.

There was something else on his radar, Neil realized—a dot approaching from behind. At first he assumed it was another aircraft headed for the USS *Martin Van Buren*, possibly to refuel, but it wasn't slowing down. It was accelerating. Acting on instinct, Neil swerved the plane hard to the right, knocking everyone against the taut safety straps of their seats.

"Andertol!" Jones bellowed in his earpiece. "What the—"

At that exact moment, a rocket shot past, missing the jet by a matter of feet and exploding in a fiery ball in the space ahead.

"That's enemy fire, recruits!" Jones boomed. "Somebody get me some eyes on who that is!"

Neil and Trevor frantically turned their heads, as Biggs and Riley did the same in the back. Among the four of them, every direction was covered.

"There be-eth an unmarked bogey, my liege," Riley replied.

"Somebody wanna tell me what he's saying?" Jones exclaimed.

"We have visual on that bogey," Neil confirmed. "Or, uh, we used to . . . ," Neil trailed off as they all watched the enemy fighter begin to shimmer invisible—almost like the Chameleon could. Neil peered closely and could still see the outline.

"They're trying to activate camouflage, but it doesn't seem to be on a par with ours," Jason 1 was saying from another plane. "Look, you can tell it's created to broadcast from only one viewing angle. If we pulled up or below, we could probably see the plane."

"You heard the kid! Pull up!" Jones yelled. "Pilots, back in command! Copilots, release controls!"

Abruptly, Trevor guided the nose of the fighter up, forcefully reclaiming the controls just as another rocket shot past them.

"Why haven't we gone invisible yet?" Neil blurted out. The plan had been to activate the invisibility technology after refueling on the *Martin Van Buren*. But when they made that plan, no one knew they were going to get shot at.

"Good thinking, Andertol," said Jones. "All Chameleons, activate camouflage. Abandon first destination and proceed directly to second coordinates. I repeat, continue on to second coordinates. You've all had enough practice!"

Biggs fired up the invisibility technology for the Chameleon, and Neil could feel it in his bones as the entire craft began to vibrate. As the formation of jets vanished into thin air, Neil hoped this was enough to shake off their strange, half-invisible enemy.

CHAPTER 11

THEY FLEW STRAIGHT AND SILENT FOR A FEW SECONDS, BUT it seemed like an hour, while the enemy fighter looped around in search of Neil and company. It ducked up and down, firing frustrated shots into the distance as it scoured the air. But as the search came up fruitless, the aircraft eventually turned around, returning in the direction they'd just come from.

Neil breathed a deep sigh of relief. They were okay. But the faint, high-pitched buzzing sound that started when the invisibility scales were fully activated was beginning to make his teeth grind. It reminded him of when the cable box was turned off at his grandparents' house while their old tube television was accidentally still on and the TV's faint screech droned incessantly. Neil was always the first to notice it, as apparently the others in his family were unable to hear the frequency. He wondered if it would be the same now, or if this meant he possessed doglike hearing.

"Sam, you getting that buzzing sound too?" Neil asked into his headset.

"What buzzing sound?" Sam sounded confused.

Uh-oh. Dog hearing is sounding more and more likely.

While Trevor maintained control of the gears, Neil wished he could check out his jet's invisibility in action. From inside the plane everything still looked normal— he could see the exteriors of the other jets, a safety feature so that the invisible planes wouldn't crash into one another. But Neil had secretly been hoping that he would at least be able to look through the floor of his jet to the ground below, like those glass floors atop tall buildings designed to lure tourists.

"That was close, recruits," Jones said, jogging Neil's attention. "I've alerted the *Martin Van Buren* to the situation, and they'll be in pursuit of the bogeys. Continue at full speed to our final destination."

"But, sir," Corinne piped up from the neighboring jet, "we haven't practiced landing!"

"I have trust in you, cadet," Jones reassured her. "Now, we're going to bring up our satellite feed to see what we're dealing with. I want all craft to stay at about thirty thousand feet for now. I'm thinking we can get a bird's-eye on our craft and just hover down nice and quiet-like."

Trevor pulled back farther on the joystick, but there was tension in the gears. He looked at Neil as if something wasn't right.

"What'd you do, Ashley?"

"What? I didn't touch anything. I haven't even been flying!" Neil responded. He grabbed hold of his controls and tried moving them, but the plane continued to level out, barely idling forward.

Uh-oh, Neil thought.

At the same time, everyone's visor display went blank. The coordinates, levels, and monitors disappeared.

"It's okay, cadets," Jones said. "Electrical systems are still operational, just not sure what's going on. Mission Control. Mission Control . . . ," Jones's voice repeated, but there was no reply. "Wells, Lopez. Switch to the alternate channel on the telecom." Neil could hear a click as they left to talk privately. Neil tried to stay calm and ignore the gnawing feeling that if something needed to be said on a separate channel, it probably wasn't good.

He returned his focus to the gauges in front of him and concentrated on getting them to their final destination. Neil was just starting to get back into the swing of things when the jet suddenly hit an air pocket. In an instant, the plane dipped, but Trevor quickly pulled back up to correct their flight. His confidence guiding the plane was impressive, but Neil had a feeling that something still wasn't right.

"Hey, Trevor," Neil said, "we should slow down a little so we don't leave a vapor trail or anything. Don't want to make being invisible pointless."

"*Psh*, I know, Ashley," Trevor replied, but he increased the speed anyway.

The invisible fighter pushed on, covering hundreds of miles of ocean in minutes. The jets skimmed over a blanket of puffy white clouds, the choppy sea appearing in the small gaps between them.

"Pilots, let's pull back a bit. If estimations are accurate, we should be getting close to our missing ship's location," said Jones, returning to the main radio channel. "Looks like we're getting continued interference on our radar, though." He slapped his helmet, and then the screens surrounding him. It was obvious Jones was not exactly familiar with the technology.

"Jones, I'd be happy to take a look at the radar. I'm wondering if there's a—" JP started to say.

"Silence, recruits," commanded Jones. He looked toward the horizon. "Due to apparent technical difficulties, we'll have to do this the old-fashioned way: with our own two eyes. On my mark, we'll hover down to scout out what's below us. If my map's correct, I'm not seeing that there should be anything, so keep your eyes out for our craft floating below. Stay in formation as best you can, pilots, and do exactly as I say. Now, let's do this."

Switching the craft's controls with a toggle of his thumb, Trevor dived toward the surface of the ocean. Neil felt his stomach get left behind at a higher altitude. They were falling fast—*too fast*, Neil thought, watching the altimeter drop from six digits to four. This was bad. Neil grabbed his controller and tried to correct Trevor's flying, pitching the nose up ever so slightly. With a free hand, he pulled back on the throttle.

- -

They slowed, but only for a moment. Neil looked to see Trevor's hand firmly on the thrust controls, pushing well beyond the speed Neil had just corrected.

The fighter burst clear from the cloud cover to loom over a small chain of three islands. Neil could see where tidal pools had carved the land, leaving sandbars and jutting rocks scattered around the row of oddly shaped landforms. There was a larger main island that formed a misshapen triangle with two smaller ones. It looked like a spooky, half-smiling face, Neil thought. Two uneven eyes above a crescent mouth.

"What's going on up there? Slow down, pilots!" Jones snapped as the jet sped down toward the smallest island. Neither of the boys responded. Neil just gritted his teeth, clutching the throttle as he tried his best to reduce Trevor's pace.

"This isn't fun and games, soldiers. Cut this out," Jones commanded.

"I can land these things on a dime in the game," Trevor insisted. "Just watch."

Neil let go, as if to say "Fine, do it your way," and immediately regretted his decision. Trevor just kept accelerating, and without Neil's resistance, they plunged even faster.

The tops of the palm trees below grew terrifyingly close, and Trevor finally tried to slow down. But he'd waited too long.

At the center of the smallest island was a tiny crater devoid of trees. Trevor aimed for it. As they neared, a subtle red glow became visible from cracks in the bottom of the rocky circle.

"Trevor, that's lava!" Neil cried out.

"Get us out of here!" Jones shouted.

The heat rising up from the small crater of magma below caused the thrusters to moan and fire out of sync. Neil felt the once-powerful fighter wobble in midair, circling unsteadily like a bad juggler's spinning plate atop a stick.

"Watch out!" Neil shrieked as dozens of gauges began to beep in distress. The Chameleon thrashed through the humid tropical air, unleashing a sputtering howl as it lost control and launched into a violent tailspin.

As they spiraled down, Neil looked for something, anything, to help. He saw a handle marked EMERGENCY and pulled it firmly, before realizing that the next word was RELEASE. Neil stayed put, but a cache of gear spilled out from the belly of the plane into a thick patch of palm trees.

In a final, disorienting plummet, the jet took a nose-dive toward the white sand beach that circled the small island.

"Thy ship is verily crashing!" Riley exclaimed.

"If anyone finds a recording of this, as my last living will and testament, I leave everything to my cat, Mayor Mittenbottom!" Biggs screamed.

"Tell that to Mayor Mittenbottom yourself," Neil replied. "We're not going down like this!" And with every ounce of strength he had, he yanked back on the throttle, forcing the tail of the jet to stabilize and breaking them free of their swirling descent. But just as he thought he might have regained control, the jet hit a tangle of vines dangling between tall palm trees and jerked to the ground.

The plane landed with a thick, powerful slap, first its tail and then its nose. Seaweed and driftwood flew in all directions, settling onto the sand like pieces of confetti. Neil's safety harness dug into his body, knocking the wind out of him. As he gasped for air, his ears were ringing at a loud and unforgiving frequency. He looked up at the blinding sun and winced.

He was in trouble. This was far, far worse than broken headgear.

CHAPTER

12

AS NEIL UNDID THE HELMET AND THE SAFETY BELT SECURED around his body, he could hear the muffled whines of the others around him. He shook his head, confirming that no bones were broken, only to grimace when Jones's voice echoed through the cockpit.

"Grunsten! Andertol! Are you trying to get us killed?" Jones fumed.

Jones yanked open the ship's glass top, hastily undoing his safety harness and slamming down his helmet. The major hopped out of the plane to survey the damage, his strong arms and legs moving like a machine.

"Out here, soldiers!" Jones yelled. The four recruits hurried to stumble out onto the fine white sand.

"Well, great. Just great," Jones began. He walked around the fighter, frowning as he surveyed the damage. Fortunately, aside from a few long scrapes and a thick vine tangled into one of the turbines, there didn't seem to be too much damage that couldn't be fixed.

Neil glanced around at their surroundings, bringing his hand up to shield his eyes from the intense sunlight. The beach they were standing on ran around the edge of the island, skirting a dense jungle in the island's center. The rim of the crater they'd flown over peeked out just above the top of the tree line. The island looked to be uninhabited, apart from large animal tracks that were sketched out onto the sand in every direction.

"Way to go, copilot," Trevor spit, turning to Neil.

"Hey, I was just trying to slow us down. You were the one going too fast," Neil replied.

"Listen up, everybody, and do exactly as I say." Jones glared at Neil and Trevor. "Diagnostics confirm the Chameleon is still operational. We just need to dig it out. Since we're here because of their little stunt, Grunsten and Andertol will go get the gear that's now made a home in the jungle. The rest of you will stick with me and help dig—and when I say dig, I mean actually dig. We'll rendezvous with the others once they've secured a location."

"Jones, I—" Neil started.

"Andertol, I don't even want to hear it. You two get moving—*now*."

In silence, Neil and Trevor slowly plodded into the lush green landscape. Behind them, Neil faintly heard Riley ask Jones how he should begin digging out their metal steed.

"Great, now I have to get lost in the woods to make up for your mistake," Trevor said. Neil did his best to ignore him and focus on their task.

As they walked farther into the shadows of the trees, a symphony of jungle noises immediately surrounded them. Tall, thin bamboo stalks stretched up all around, and birds of nearly infinite species squawked and warbled. Vines hung sporadically like tossed limp noodles. Huge trees cast cool shadows, while monstrous ferns and giant-leafed plants filled in the space on the jungle floor. Neil could barely see much farther than a few trees ahead of him and had to zigzag through the forest, making his way slowly ahead.

"I think the gear dropped down not too far from here," Neil said, trying to get his bearings. Trevor just shrugged.

They walked on in silence. But soon Neil heard a rustling from the bushes behind them. He shivered, all his senses on edge, and paused as Trevor crept slowly forward. The noise grew closer. It was footsteps, Neil realized. Somebody was following them.

"Trevor, run!" yelled Neil, and the two of them took off, bobbing between massive trees that looked like dinosaur legs. Neil turned back to see who was after them, but he got only a faint glimpse before whipping his head back around to duck under a low-hanging branch. *It couldn't be*, he thought. And yet he could have sworn that they were being stalked by an ostrich.

Just as Neil turned to look back again, he and Trevor collided in a small clearing where a small patch of daylight was shining through the spaces between the palm leaves overhead.

"Watch it!" yelled Trevor.

"No, ostrich!" Neil shouted back.

"Whatrich?" Trevor responded as his foot caught on something, and suddenly, in a flurry of green and brown leaves, he and Neil were yanked up and away from the jungle floor, engulfed in a handmade net of vines. They squirmed together, human pretzels in organic netting.

"How did you not see the trip wire?" Neil yelled in frustration as he looked over to see a tree house perched high in the nearby trees. A makeshift ladder was secured to one side. He scanned the ground below for any signs of its inhabitant.

"Whoever made this doesn't know what's about to happen to them," Trevor fumed. "When my dad hears about this—well, let's just say it'll be a new record for a lawsuit on net-related trauma!"

"Dude! We're in a net!" Neil snapped. "Your dad can't help us right now. We need to figure out how we'll actually get out of here!"

Neil reached for the vines encasing them and tried to rip them apart, but they were sturdy and thick, almost as wide as the climbing rope in his gym class.

"Do you have a Swiss Army knife or anything?" Neil asked, thinking of ways to cut themselves free.

"Um, *no*," Trevor said.

Neil rolled his eyes and tried to examine his surroundings some more, but with his body stuck at a sixty-degree angle and his head jutted to the side, it was difficult to see much. Pushing his head through a small hole in the netting, Neil ratcheted his head to the left as far as possible. In the distance he could just see the cache of gear and food they'd dropped, and something else.

Out of the woods, a shadowy figure appeared behind their gear, lumbering slowly toward them. Neil caught his breath in panic. "Trevor . . . ," Neil whispered, "someone's coming!"

CHAPTER

13

THE TREE HOLDING NEIL AND TREVOR CREAKED SUBTLY WITH their weight as they swayed back and forth twenty feet in the air. Rays of yellow sunlight leaked in splattered patches through the canopy of leaves. Neil twisted to see the figure as it approached, but the person remained shapeless, still nestled in shadows. Neil closed his eyes, bracing himself for the worst; but after a few long, uneventful moments, he opened them again and saw only a boy, maybe fourteen years old, standing right below them.

"Hey!" Neil shouted. "Can you help us out? We stepped on some booby trap and ended up here!"

"Shhh!" Trevor nudged Neil in the ribs. "This thing could be his!"

Oh no . . . Trevor might actually be right, Neil thought. Neil looked down at the boy, who, smiling lazily, was taking sips from a coconut in his hand. He wore sunglasses, a dirty white captain's hat over his mess of dark hair, and khaki shorts with a thick leather belt, held by a gold clasp. He was shirtless, and his shoulders and arms looked strong, probably from tree climbing.

The boy looked up at them a bit longer, then tipped his hat and slowly started to climb the ladder to the tree house made of bamboo, straw, and trees without their bark.

"Hey!" Neil called out. "What do you want from us?" The boy didn't respond and eventually reached the thick wooden platform suspended high above the ground. He walked into the house without looking back.

"Help! Help us!" Trevor shouted while trying to squeeze an arm through a small opening in the netting, but he quickly gave up. "Jones! Jones!"

Neil rolled his eyes. They were too far away from

the beach for their voices to carry. He scoured the net for a point of weakness that they could use to escape, but there was nothing. Trevor was still yelling, his voice beginning to rasp.

"Save your energy, Trevor. I don't think they can hear us," Neil said.

"I'll use my energy however I want to," Trevor snapped.

Neil had tried his best with Trevor, but now that they were smashed together in a vine-woven net, he couldn't let Trevor get away with his jerky comments anymore.

"Listen," Neil said. "I know you don't like me, man, and the feeling is mutual, but we're in this together, for better or worse. Look around—we're stuck in a freaking *net*, and you're acting like you always do. I know how you are during games."

"What does that mean?" Trevor asked, turning his net-squeezed face away from Neil.

"You only look out for yourself!" Neil thought of how Trevor had flown in the simulator, how he had climbed up Neil on the Decider.

"Because why bother with the rest of you when I know I'm better?"

"You're wrong," said Neil.

"*I'm* wrong? I feel sorry for you, Ashley. You always pair up with losers like Sam and Biggs when you could be so much more. Why do you think you're still second in the standings? If you stopped playing team games with all the mediocre gamers, you might have a chance. You're actually pretty good. But you're letting them hold you back."

"Watch it," Neil snapped. Trevor could insult him all he wanted, but he refused to let him bad-mouth his friends.

"You know you're better than them. Admit it."

Before Neil could respond, a rustling sound came from inside the tree house and he turned to look. Through the lone window, he saw something flicker, and then he heard the distinct buzz of a tube television.

"Trevor, look!" Neil exclaimed, pointing a finger. Trevor arched backward to see. The small television in the tree house was playing *Wheel of Fortune*, one of Neil's favorite shows. The boy inside plopped down on a wooden chair and began to watch as white spaces for letters lit up the screen.

Neil thought furiously. Every morning before school

for the last three years, he'd watched the show while being force-fed oatmeal by his mother. He could guess every puzzle with no more than two or three letters provided and knew what kind of spinning finesse was required to land on the $2,500 space.

Neil leaned forward in the net as a jubilant woman named Sherry shouted *"L!"*

"THE LEGEND OF SLEEPY HOLLOW!" Neil proclaimed before all the *L*s even lit up the board. The boy inside looked surprised and glanced over at Neil and Trevor, then turned up the volume. He watched as Sherry bought more vowels than necessary and then promptly went bankrupt. A truck driver named Thad solved the puzzle, needing five more letters than Neil.

The same continued with the next round, with Neil shouting out "UMBRELLA STAND AND DELIVER!" The boy turned again, possibly impressed with Neil's *Wheel* prowess.

As the final round neared and a botanist named Cecilia hoped to leave in a Hyundai or something, Neil had an idea.

"Hey!" he shouted. "I get this puzzle before you, and you let us down. If not, we stay in the net. Sound fair?"

The boy didn't respond but was intently watching Cecilia guess if the final puzzle, a "thing," contained *W, X, F,* or *Y.*

Truly awful choices, Cecilia, Neil thought.

With only _ _ S_ _ _ _N to work with, Neil's mind scrambled to fill in the spaces. As seconds ticked by, it finally clicked.

"OBSIDIAN!" Neil shouted with a satisfied grin. He heard the boy in the tree house holler the same answer a second later, and he watched Cecilia recoil as her time ran out, frowning at a shimmery envelope worth $30,000.

The boy flipped off the television screen and slowly walked outside to the creaky wooden deck. He reached up to a vine in front of his house and pulled, sending Neil and Trevor to the ground in a clump. Then he grabbed a second vine and promptly did a looping swing to land next to Trevor and Neil, who were now scrabbling with the net, searching for an opening. The boy's bare feet hit the ground lightly, leaving graceful footprints in the spongy, moss-covered dirt.

"I'm glad to see the adjustments worked. Last time they got away," said the boy.

Last time? They? Neil thought it best to ask as few

questions as possible. Just being out of the net was a step in the right direction, and he didn't want to press his luck.

"Um, hi. I'm Neil," he began. "And this is—"

"Kenny. Kenny Boseswich," Trevor said, cutting Neil off. He held out his hand for a handshake.

"Sorry about that," said the boy. "The surf doesn't break that well over on this side of the chain. You must be pretty lost if you're on this island."

"Yeah, we just sort of dropped in," Neil said. "Maybe you could show us around?" Neil thought if he returned to Jones with some reconnaissance information as well as their gear, it might help get him out of hot water.

"Sure," the boy said with a shrug as he spun away quickly and started into the wilderness. "Least I can do for the capturing thing. I'm Weo, by the way."

Neil followed Weo as Trevor hung back. The three stepped over dark soil, at times walking on the tops of roots that trickled out from trees in every direction.

"If we can get to high enough ground, I bet we can see where that Chameleon is," Trevor whispered from the corner of his mouth. "It's gotta be on one of these islands."

"I doubt it. It's invisible," Neil reminded him as he followed Weo. "But yeah, maybe we can get an idea."

Weo cut through the jungle instinctively, moving much faster than Neil and Trevor had on their own. Occasionally he paused and touched the rough exterior of a palm tree or giant leaf with the tips of his fingers. Neil did the same, wondering if doing so would reveal jungle secrets.

They soon reached the base of the small crater that Trevor had almost crashed their jet into earlier. The lush jungle plants gave way to glossy black rocks of all sizes, reflecting back the intense sun. Weo scooped down to pick up two fallen coconuts and cracked open the tops on a large volcanic rock. He handed one each to Trevor and Neil. At first they hesitated, but after the first sip, they drank greedily. The liquid inside was smooth and refreshing.

"Wow, that was great. Thanks," Neil said, wiping his mouth. Neil mentally added fresh coconut to the list of things he enjoyed drinking, which so far only included chocolate milk: extra chocolate, less milk.

The three traipsed up the small rocky incline and soon looked out over the beautiful scenery. To the right was the largest island, white-capped waves lapping at its shore. Two surfers sat on foam boards a distance out, waiting to time their ride in. Small, makeshift buildings dotted the coastline.

To the left, and closer, was the third island, only slightly larger than the one they were currently standing on. Shards of black volcanic rock jutted from the ocean, and a thin ring of trees lined the outside. At its center, a giant modern gray building surrounded by a metal fence sat firmly planted in the otherwise rugged surroundings. A new-looking suspension bridge connected that island to the bigger island, leaving the small island that Neil was on completely secluded.

"So, what do you call this place?" Neil asked, shielding his eyes from the sun. Weo gave a short laugh.

"Well, there's the main island," Weo said, pointing to the biggest one. "The old top-secret surf spot. Unreal waves. I guess some people call it Brosiah Bay now," Weo explained.

"Brosiah Bay?" Trevor asked.

"Goofy, I know. It's a surf term, sort of. But now lots of nonsurfers live there, too."

"Cool," Neil responded. "And that other island. With

all the rocks and that building. What's that?"

Weo's tone quickly changed. "That . . . that island is the . . . Well, it belongs to . . . Let's just say it's best to leave the billionaire alone."

Billionaire? Neil gasped. *That's unreal—a private island. I bet the floors are made of precious metals, and there's a video arcade, which is just off the bowling alley, next to a hangar full of motorcycles and jets . . . just like the missing . . .* "Chameleon!" Neil said aloud. Weo turned his attention to Neil.

"Really? Where? I haven't seen those on my island before."

"Oh, yeah. Just found one. Tre—Kenny . . . ah, Ghostswitch . . . I've found our sample chameleon," Neil said, doing a pretty awful job of playing it cool. "We can return back to the gear for sampling purposes."

Trevor met Neil's gaze in understanding. "Yeeeah . . . ," Trevor said slowly. "We should get back."

"Can I see it?"

"Well, Weo, great meetin' ya and all, but we've got important scientist stuff to attend to. That's what we are; I forgot to tell you. Scientists. Surf-loving scientists. Obviously the chameleon is camouflaged on my friend's body here, so we can't disturb it. That's the first rule of surf science!" Neil said, slapping Weo on the back.

"Yeah, what he said," Trevor blurted. "Any chance you can lead us back to our gear?"

Weo narrowed his eyes but simply nodded and turned back around, clambering down the path on the tough soles of his bare feet. Neil hated lying, especially to someone who had just released him from a net, but they needed to go tell Jones about the billionaire's island. And Weo had put them up in that tree anyway.

"There's the gear," Trevor said as he saw their pile of bags in the same clearing as before. He scurried ahead, making sure to step well over Weo's trip wire.

After helping position the bags on Neil's and Trevor's flimsy shoulders, Weo quickly gave them directions to the beach, with a wide variety of landmarks to search for. They all had weird names, like "snake mountain" and "dung beetle waterslide."

"Thanks, Weo." Neil adjusted the black duffel bag of gear on his scrawny right shoulder and started after Trevor. He'd taken only a few steps when Weo called after him.

"Hey, Neil? This tree house and everything? Let's keep it our secret. But if you run into any of the ostriches, to get them to chill out, make a sound like . . . what's the word? Like you're choking on a sandwich that you made with too much peanut butter!" Weo shouted, climbing the ladder back up to his tree fort.

Neil nodded and plodded ahead, following Weo's bizarre instructions. He made a left at the first tree shaped like a Y and then a right at the "old man's face rock," and by the time he had walked too far to go back, he realized that he had absolutely no idea what that ostrich noise would sound like.

CHAPTER

14

NEIL FELL INTO A SORT OF GALLOP, BALANCING THE cumbersome bag on his hips while hop-running. He tried to keep his eyes on Trevor but at times just looked for the imprints of his thick government-issued shoes. The footprints led through leaves and crawling roots, back to the beach and their group of soldiers.

By the time he reached the edge of the forest, Neil saw from a distance that the Chameleon was nearly free of sand.

"Lord Jones, your soot-colored, burlap-sacked

textiles have arrived," said Riley, pointing toward Neil and Trevor. Jones's head popped up from the opposite side of the Chameleon, the late-afternoon sun reflecting on his forehead. He looked like some kind of sand-dwelling creature crawling out of a newly dug tunnel. By the noticeable amount of sweat drenching him, Neil thought it was safe to assume that Jones had done most of the work.

"Oh, thanks for really hustling with everything, gentlemen." Jones moaned, spitting out sand. "I've enjoyed digging us out with Spineyard here while Starshine over there took it easy."

"Again, 'tis not me name. I am but a humble *swine-herd*, and at your service, my most revered Jones," said Riley. "And we are sentinels on lookout, a very necessary outpost indeed."

"Never mind," Jones said brusquely. "Fortunately the radios with Lopez and Wells still work, and the others are setting up a base camp. They're at an old, abandoned farm on the bigger island. Now that you're back, we can get moving."

Neil and Trevor returned the dropped gear to the fighter, trying to avoid eye contact with Jones. Neil wanted to tell the major what he'd found out about the billionaire's island, but he could see that this was not the time. Biggs and Riley then hopped in, sand flying off their clothes and shoes.

"Oh, come on, not in the interior!" Jones yelled. "Were you raised by longshoremen?"

"No, wolves. Remember?" Biggs said sheepishly.

Everyone mumbled apologies and quickly buckled in as the cockpit sealed shut. Biggs typed something into the invisibility command, and soon the plane was clad in its invisible facade.

"Good-bye, weird-smells island," Biggs said with a smile. "Not sure what kind of animal droppings you smell like, but I swear to you now, I will re-create it for television. Even if it takes all my free time. That is a promise."

Trevor lifted the craft up and out of its embankment, whirling up sand on the beach below. Neil heard the high-pitched buzz of the invisible exterior, and behind that, so faint it almost wasn't audible, a slight whir he hadn't heard earlier.

"Humidity makes these thrusters a little noisy," Jones said. "Grunsten, take us up slowly. We'll head to the southeast corner of the other island. You should hopefully see the barn where our team has taken shelter. On our mark, they'll open the back doors, and we can idle in unnoticed."

"Roger that," Trevor replied.

The invisible fighter glided across the water, tracing the edge of what Weo had called Brosiah Bay. Waves lapped below them, and wormlike ribbons of sandbars twisted in and out of the water. Trevor soon cut over the land, which was dotted with symmetrical plants, all in uniform rows.

"Hmm. Looks to be pineapples," Jones said.

"These apples of pine, O Jones—they grow from the loam beneath our feet?" Riley asked.

"Pineapples grow from the ground, if that's what you're asking in whatever accent and language that is. Now, Grunsten, you see that barn ahead? That's our destination," Jones said. Trevor steered toward an ancient, decrepit barn, its browned and splintering slats all leaning at an eighty-degree angle.

Steering wide of the farmer's house at the opposite end of the plot of land, Trevor landed the Chameleon softly on the ground and crept in silently between the open barn doors, like a battle-ready Prius. He slowed the jet to a stop and pressed the button to open the cockpit, which unlatched with a pleasing *whoosh*.

As Neil disembarked, he glanced over at Wells and Lopez, who were standing at attention while the rest of the crew sat transfixed, watching a documentary on historical obstacle courses being displayed on the exterior of one of the other Chameleons. That was definitely one of the coolest perks of the jet's video-camouflaging technology, Neil thought. A few kids from the other planes lay underneath the belly of the fighter, taking in a film many times their size.

Neil looked up from the underside of the plane to see Sam, watching from the auxiliary seat in the open cockpit.

"Hey, Sam," Neil said, moving closer as she climbed down from the jet.

"Neil," Sam said, her voice just above a whisper. "Everything okay? You were gone for a while."

"Oh, yeah." Neil said, feeling his ears grow red. "Just your classic net inci—"

"All right, soldiers," Jones said, interrupting Neil and the movie everyone was enjoying. "Wells, Lopez, and I are headed for recon and to see if we can get our communication to the aircraft carrier restored. We think whatever knocked it out in the air is still keeping a signal from getting to us. All of you just stay here. Only rule is nobody leaves the barn. Period."

Neil realized this was his chance to make sure Jones at least heard his intelligence on the islands. "Major Jones, before you leave, you should—"

"Save it for later, Andertol. I need you, especially after last time, to just not touch anything."

Jones turned and slipped out through the swaying back doors. Wells and Lopez followed, silent as ever. The doors shut, and then they were gone.

"Do those guys ever talk?" Trevor asked.

"Wells and Lopez? Now that I think about it, hardly at all," Jason 1 said. Sam and Corinne turned in to form a circle, both of them nodding in agreement.

"Yeah, we're actually wondering if it's a competition between them to see who can talk less. Or if they're just cyborgs," said Corinne, who spoke with a nasally confidence.

"Wells is a robot for sure. I don't think he's even said a word to us," Sam said. "And I watched him do three hundred push-ups in a row, which I'm pretty sure can't be done by a human."

"Lopez is all about extended periods without eye blinking," Corinne said. "Count in your head next time and try not to feel your eyes get scratchy. Terrifying."

The twelve kids formed a jagged oval, anxiously talking to one another.

"Were you saying something about a net?" Sam asked Neil to the side. "What were you talking about earlier?"

"Well, we took, uh, a detour. On descent, I *misplaced* our gear from the plane. But we got to see the other islands around here," Neil said, feeling his armpits begin to sweat again. "There's a big fortress-type thing on one of them—metal fence, secured entrance. Apparently owned by a billionaire. Even looks big enough to hold a stolen jet . . . just saying."

"Dude!" Biggs's voice cut in. "We're settling this old school." He and the others were still arguing over which soldier was more of a cyborg. "Team Lopez on this side,

Team Wells on the other. Somebody get a rope. It's tug-of-war time."

★ ★ ★

The sun was almost fully set, and a few shoulders nearly dislocated, when Jones, Wells, and Lopez returned with news. A wireless grid had been set up around the islands, blocking all communication or radio to the outside world. Any outgoing signals were completely trapped.

"In this darkness and without any communication, we won't be able to do much, soldiers. The place is swarming with guards. So we're staying here for the night. From what Wells and Lopez intercepted earlier, we still know the general location of our men and plane. They're in a warehouse on a separate island in the chain."

That was my discovery, Neil thought, feeling a little validated that today hadn't totally been for naught.

"We leave at oh-five-hundred tomorrow morning. We'll have dinner now and then it's lights-out," Jones said.

After sitting in a circle for dinner and prodding their MREs—meals ready to eat, each of which consisted of a lukewarm plastic bag of fake beef—everyone crawled into their emergency blankets. Each recruit had been given a crinkly silver square, mainly used for survival or in case of a fire, but when unfolded, it provided immense heat without much weight or thickness. If he hadn't been lying on a dirty barn floor, Neil probably would have been pretty cozy. Jones, Wells, and Lopez laid their blankets near the barn's exit to make sure no one got in—or out.

★ ★ ★

After an hour, the soldiers in command were sound asleep, their breathing loud. They looked so comfortable, Neil thought they must be trained for sleeping in unfamiliar terrain. Jones snored—loudly. He sounded like two hungry, vicious possums fighting over food. At times it even seemed as if a third was getting into the mix.

The snoring unceasing, Sam slowly crawled between bodies over to Neil.

"You awake?" she asked softly.

"Yeah," Neil replied.

"What do you think that is?" Sam cupped her hand around her ear. Through the splintered slats of the barn, Neil and Sam heard chanting, or music of some kind. It started out softly, but it was soon clear that whatever it was, was only going to grow louder.

"I think we should go check it out," she said.

"I don't know. I mean, we're not supposed to leave here. And what if it's, like, something dangerous?" Neil replied.

"Oh, come on," Sam urged in a convincing tone Neil remembered from countless games. "Besides, how are we gonna have any luck sleeping with hacksaw Jones here?"

She did have a point. Neil did wonder if at some point in the night, local wildlife might try to see what type of animal sounded like it was struggling for life inside the confines of the withered barn.

But before Neil could throw off his crinkly blanket, Biggs darted upright like a movie monster brought to life. He cocked his head and listened for barely a second before peeling off his emergency blanket. He groaned like a zombie hungry for a midnight brain snack.

"Hey, Biggs," Neil whispered, but Biggs didn't respond. He walked to the side of the door opposite Jones, where a wide wooden slat was loose, and pulled at its sides.

"Biggs, slow down, man. What's up?" Neil asked his friend. Biggs still said nothing, and with another tug at the barn's ancient carpentry, he had made a hole just big

- -

enough for him to crawl through.

"Druuuaa . . . .mmmsss buh . . . buhongo . . . ," Biggs mumbled, and slipped outside.

Neil and Sam turned to each other. "I mean, we can't just let him go alone, can we?" Sam asked. Neil knew she was right. Maybe Biggs was a sleepwalker? Or maybe his body, after years of vegetarianism, just got up in the middle of the night to find the nearest steak?

"Okay," Neil half whispered reluctantly.

He quickly tied his shoes, trying his best to be quiet, but everyone else was rustled awake in the process. Most had never fallen asleep, likely unable to tune out the sonic assault of Jones's deviated septum. The others looked up from their makeshift beds, eyes blinking in confusion.

"Hey, guys," Neil whispered to the rest of the crew, "Biggs just stumbled outside, sleepwalking. We're gonna go make sure he's okay. You comin'?"

Before Neil had even finished talking, everyone was already stealthily tying their shoes too. Sam propped open the rickety slat on the side of the barn, exposing a huge bonfire in the distance, and made her way outside.

Neil peeked his head out of the opening, took a

deep breath, and then wiggled through. Staring out in the distance at the rows of pineapples and his sleepwalking zombie friend, Neil crept into the night, uncertain of what was in store.

CHAPTER

15

★ ★ ★

NEIL HAD NEVER SEEN SO MANY STARS. THE NIGHT SKY WAS bold and unending, brighter than he'd ever seen it at home. The stars all scattered in every direction as if they'd been thrown, two-handed, from a basket.

The light of their glow grew fainter as Neil got closer to the roaring fire at the island's center. The group of recruits approached it carefully, moving forward slowly over the spongy and thick grass. The fire was magnetic, sending sparks popping with dark orange-and-blue flames. Near the fire's edge, Neil spotted the shadow of his sleepwalking friend staggering toward the glowing embers. People were circling around the large bonfire in a flurry of claps, yips, and yelps, all tossing logs and huge pieces of driftwood onto the blaze.

"Biggs! *Psst*, Biggs!" Neil shouted, but his friend continued on, stumbling hazily around a dark cluster of trees. Neil raced after him, turning the corner and running into the back of a hulking local. He and a few others had formed a circle around Biggs.

"Hey, stop! Biggs, run!" Neil yelled, assuming this was some kind of midnight brainwashing.

Neil tried squirming through the wall of strangers to break his friend loose, but it was like fighting a losing game of red rover. And then, suddenly, the circle broke open on its own, and Biggs emerged from the center, his shirt and signature cap now replaced by a small bongo drum, a fringed leather vest, and what looked to be a plastic toy ostrich beak over his nose.

"Neil! It's a drum circle, my man!" Biggs exclaimed, now completely awake. He slapped the tops of the drums, and a thousand-watt smile stretched across his face.

Neil smiled, relieved. "I was worried you were gonna sleepwalk right into the fire or something."

- -

"Nah. Sorry if I scared ya, though. I do have a history of sleep-drumming, and I have a way of finding these types of things. It's, like, my sixth, possibly seventh, sense," Biggs said as he tapped out a simple beat. "And thanks for coming to find me, Neil. That means a lot. And since I'm journal-less, if I get inspired to dictate some of the smells I encounter, would you mind trying to jot 'em down?"

"Sure thing." Neil shrugged.

The rest of the group shuffled around the bend of trees, heading in their direction.

"Dudes!" Biggs waved over the rest of their new friends as they sheepishly walked around the edge of the circle, the rise and fall of drumbeats filling the warm night air. Strangers with sunburns and beads in their hair greeted the group, offering tambourines and thin, plastic glowing jewelry, the kind that look like straws with ends that snapped together. Getting into the spirit of things, Neil grabbed a neon-yellow glow bracelet and put it on. The other kids—all gamers in the truest sense, and therefore fans of loud noises and a blatant disregard for curfews—seemed equally entranced by the drum circle.

Sam grabbed Neil's wrist, and they cut through the

outer ring of people, followed by Yuri and the two Jasons.

"We have a bonfire at my boarding school," Yuri said, putting his hands on Jason 1's shoulders like people do on a conga line. "It's the closing ceremony for our geometry Olympics."

The ring of people kept turning, a mess of noise amplifying in all directions.

"Guys, I've got a good chant we can do," said Jason 1. "You ever play Uncle Tony's Pro Football Dynasty? They have this chant the crowd does—"

But Jason 1 was cut off by a local girl wearing a tie-dyed headband and an ostrich beak similar to the one Biggs had on. Her short, matted hair was still damp with salt water.

"Did you say 'Uncle Tony's Football'?"

"Yeah, I love it! You have it here? I could go for a game right now," Jason 1 said, his voice squeaking with hope.

"Maybe later. My friend has a copy in his surf shanty. Top secret, though, since only one game's allowed on the island," she replied. "We've been playing every week. Trying to catch this kid in first place. He's been unstoppable."

--

Jason 1 blushed and stayed silent as he and the girl edged into the ring of drummers closest to the fire. Neil shrugged, following along, while Jason 2 and Yuri lagged behind, busy seeing how many glowing bracelets they could link together. Drums, cymbals, bells, and tambourines had started to find their way into the fireside orchestra. Neil even thought he heard a gong banging somewhere. Soon, though, Neil began to feel the crowd closing in, and heat of the fire started to get to him.

"Want to take a break?" Neil asked his fellow recruits, and the others nodded. Neil quickly ducked out of the circle to sit cross-legged in an open patch of grass. Yuri, Jason 1, and Jason 2 were right behind him.

"Man, that was great," said Jason 1, staring up at the tiki torches in the grass.

"And I heard that girl talking about that game," Neil said. "Aren't you the guy in first place?"

"Yeah, I try to play it cool, though," Jason 1 said sheepishly. "Most people just want to challenge you right there on the spot, so I tend not to bring it up."

"Yeah," Neil said quietly, running his fingers through his hair, just grazing over his almost-forgotten bald spots. "So do you know where everybody else is?"

"Hey, man! Don't just sit there. You gotta join in," said a local in light-blue board shorts, his chest painted sparkly silver.

"We just got out of— I mean—we're good," Yuri answered.

"Here, play this," the guy said, handing a mahogany bongo drum to Neil.

"Well, okay. Thanks. Hey, so is this Brosiah Bay?" Neil asked, remembering what Weo had said earlier.

"Sure is!" the stranger replied, and danced off toward the fire.

Neil then saw some of the other recruits still in the crowd and tried to wave them over. Soon JP, Corinne, Waffles, and Dale joined them, creating a big circle in the grass.

"Music truly is the universal language," Biggs said as he walked up, his neck surrounded by roughly thirty-seven glowing rings.

"I beg to differ!" shouted JP. "Binary! Numbers!"

Before Biggs could utter a worthy debate response, a ball of flame shot into the air from the fire pit, illuminating them in light so bright that, for a split second, it seemed like daylight.

"Now, let's do this the *right* way!" Waffles shouted, arranging four drums from smallest to largest. "You guys like that game Professional Musician: Loud Noises Edition?"

"Yeah, man!" yelled Biggs.

"I'm going to a tournament next month. This will be good practice!" said Waffles.

"Awesome!" Biggs exclaimed. "Circle of positive energy time! Show us what you got!"

"Circle of what?" Waffles asked, spinning each drum to secure it in the thick grass.

"Positive energy! Good-time vibes! Everybody has to contribute! You first!"

Without needing any further urging, Waffles began flailing his arms like two electrified noodles. Then he started to play in a flurry of rhythm, eventually building a solid tempo that switched between the two drums in front of his bent knees. He looked up at the group surrounding him. "Come on, guys!" he yelled, still frantically pounding at the drums. "Who's next?"

Biggs stepped into the center of the circle. He produced a hacky sack from his pocket and kicked it three times, the last time high up in the air. It landed perfectly in the center of his forehead. He grabbed the beanbag from his head and bowed, hopping out of the circle's center. His eyes went to Neil, but Neil quickly looked away. An impromptu dance party wasn't something he'd prepared for.

Instead, Corinne jumped in, moving in some kind of dance that Neil had never seen before: fast, fluid movements slowly turning into short, jerky, machinelike dancing. She tossed her head from side to side, her shoulders rolling in different directions, her arms robotically chopping in short bursts.

Then Jason 2, with drumbeats and claps all around him, walked to the center of the group, set his feet, and leaned forward. "I used to take tumbling classes," he said before executing a perfect backflip. Nailing a flawless landing, he brought his head up with the aplomb of an Olympian. The crowd around him, growing bigger as more of the locals joined the gamers, all cheered as loudly as they could.

"I think that's gonna get him through to the next round, Bob!" Biggs exclaimed, holding an imaginary sportscaster microphone in front of his mouth.

Neil turned to Corinne, who'd moved next to him

in the circle and was still swaying in that way he couldn't place. "You seem so . . . familiar?" he blurted out.

"Semaphore," she replied, shouting over the commotion.

"Huh?"

"S-E-M-A-P-H-O-R-E," she said, contorting her body to look like each letter she was saying. "National Good Old Spelling Bee Champion five years back. I'm the child, well, prodigy from that video."

"Wow, that's you? Of course I know your video," Neil exclaimed. "You've got, like, nine million views on YouTube." He couldn't believe it. She was basically a celebrity.

"So you won that spelling bee thing?" Biggs said, overhearing them. "Is it true that when you win, they give you a secret page from the back of the dictionary with words no one has ever heard of?"

"Maybe," Corinne replied. "Top secret, though. If I told you, I'd have to . . . Let's just say I can't tell you."

Just then, Sam jumped into the middle of the circle and grabbed Neil's elbow, pulling him inside. Neil hesitated, but she smiled at him reassuringly. Against his better judgment, and neglecting his personal track record of embarrassment inside circles of humans, Neil followed.

Sam lifted the end of an extinguished tiki torch and held it out toward Neil. He grabbed on, realizing what Sam wanted to do, and held the stick at chest level.

"Limbo!" Sam and Neil both shouted. They looked at each other and smiled.

Maybe he *could* be friends with a girl, Neil realized in surprise as a line of euphoric island surfers started to form.

As Neil and Sam led the group in a round of "how low can they go," Trevor and Riley came running up in a hurry.

"Hither, my brothers in arms, lend me your ears! We have discovered ye olde za shop!" Riley proclaimed, wheezing and out of breath. "And the midnight oil of the piesmith burns long into this perfect eve!"

"Huh?" said pretty much everybody.

"We found a pizza place. It's still open. Let's go!" Trevor translated. Neil's stomach growled hungrily in response.

Abandoning the limbo game, he and the others

followed Trevor and Riley out of the packed crowd and saw a welcoming, warm orange sign in the distance that read PENELOPE'S ISLAND PIZZA. It hung over a fairly large building, which was made of natural wood and reeds. It didn't look like any pizzeria Neil had ever seen, but after a day of military training, flying, and eating MREs, he nearly sprinted inside.

CHAPTER 16

IF YOU DON'T LIKE IT, THEN DON'T EAT IT. BUT I'M STILL CHARGING YOU.

These were the first words painted atop the menu above the counter of Penelope's. Inside the place, there were two sturdy wooden tables accompanied by benches that ran the length of the room. On the left side of the restaurant was the counter to place and pick up orders and watch pizzas being baked, and on the right was an old-school-style stand-up arcade game, although the game itself looked too recent for it to be vintage. Its bright lights still flickered with life. A few kids milled around it, but no one was playing it.

A woman with long, braided hair stood behind the counter, an old orange-and-white bandanna tied loosely around her head. Her red T-shirt was dusted with flour, and she was holding a massive egg in one hand. Neil thought it looked fake, nearly twenty times the size of a regular egg. She moved in swaying motions, like she was humming a song to herself.

Neil slowly walked toward the counter, his eyes locked on the menu above. The pizzas came in three sizes—small, medium, and large—and the toppings were equally as limited, with only spinach, pineapple, and extra pineapple.

"You can keep lookin', but what's on there isn't gonna change," said the lady with the egg. Her voice lilted with an accent Neil couldn't place.

"Are those the only toppings?" Neil asked, still looking up at the sign. "Can I just get a plain cheese?"

"Well, then, you can make your own pizza place, build your own oven, and bake your own cheese pizza. I'm Penny, and so far this is the only pizza place on the island, Mr. Plain Cheese." Following Neil's gaze—he was still staring at the egg in her hand—the woman shrugged. "We just started serving ostrich egg omelets, but they're only available for breakfast. You'd have to come back in the morning for that." She had mischievous eyes but a smile that seemed comforting.

"Weird. I just saw my first ostrich," Neil said. "I think it belonged to a guy named We—" Neil stopped abruptly, remembering how Weo had asked Neil to keep his island home a secret. Penny looked surprised and sharpened her attention on Neil.

"Don't worry, sonny. I keep Weo's secrets over there on Ostrich Island," Penny said, and began kneading pizza dough. "Every day at noon he delivers the eggs fresh and takes a pizza in exchange. We both figure it's a good deal." She laughed. "Okay, Mr. Plain Cheese. You go sit down and get ready for the best pineapple pizza you've ever tasted in your life."

"The *only* pineapple pizza I've tasted in my life," Neil muttered.

"The biggest pineapple pizza we've got, with extra pineapple and a side of grilled pineapple. Coming your way, Mr. Plain Cheese."

Neil took a seat at one of the long, glossy-coated wooden tables. His eyes were soon drawn back to the video game in the corner of the restaurant. He didn't recognize it, but it was colorful and intriguing, covered in pictures of ostriches and their giant speckled eggs. *What's with all the ostriches around here?* Neil thought.

FEATHER DUSTER read the name on the console. From the description, the game promised high stakes, action, and "controls so lifelike, you'll even smell like an ostrich." Neil thought Biggs might like that aspect.

"Anybody up for a game?" Neil asked the group of recruits. Sam, Yuri, and JP all immediately volunteered.

"Oh, yeah . . . Feather Duster. I remember hearing about this—it was supposed to be great but got pulled off the market," said Yuri. "I wonder why."

The four each positioned themselves behind a player station of two buttons and a joystick. They all firmed their grip on the joysticks—which were shaped like ostrich heads, their beaks pointed at the monitor—and pressed start. The screen went black, and an ostrich egg appeared before each player. Neil could feel the familiar tingling of excitement stirring in his stomach he got whenever he played a game for the first time.

The game's camera perspective zoomed out to show a giant maze with egg-shaped holes serving as targets. Neil set off, guiding his egg past treacherous edges and dead ends. If he could roll it into one of the holes, he'd be promoted to the next level. But no matter the force he applied to the controls, he could only manage to make his egg wobble slowly forward.

"I thought this was a racing game," JP said, sounding annoyed after barely thirty seconds of unsteady egg teetering. "I'm gonna go wait for my pizza."

Neil, Sam, and Yuri decided to keep playing, and all three challengers made it through the first level. Neil figured out that by finessing the controls instead of slamming them with all his strength, he could get the egg to roll where he needed it to go. Level two opened up to reveal the same exact course, but with more obstacles.

"Seriously? The same thing? This is so boring," Sam said, bailing from the game, too.

"Yeah? I don't know. It's a little slow, but I kind of like it," Neil replied. He hated giving up on a game before he knew all its secrets. "Come get me when the pizza's here."

"That's the only game on the island, and it's a piece of junk," commented a local, who was finishing a slice of pizza. He licked his fingers and wiped them with a napkin, throwing it in the trash before heading outside.

Neil and Yuri continued to play, making it past levels three and four. Finally, in level five, their eggs both hatched into young ostriches that lived on a small farm. As Neil's ostrich reached the farm's entry gate, he met an older ostrich named Wayoh, who explained that Neil's bird could learn tricks to receive treats. It taught Neil how to execute a backflip, which Neil promptly executed for extra points. *Maybe this game isn't so bad after all*, Neil thought.

Biggs sauntered into the pizza place, at last coming in from the bonfire. "Whoa, nice going, ManofNeil," he said, coming over to see what Neil and Yuri were up to. Neil was already halfway toward setting a new record. Biggs leaned over Neil's shoulder and watched as Neil paid a second visit to Wayoh, where he learned another game secret.

"*Psst*, kid. Meet me here later if you want to get off this farm and into the races," said the grizzled old bird. Neil would be the only challenger racing, though. Yuri had given up, choosing the option that allowed his feathered avatar to retire to Ostrich Island, which offered an unending supply of things to peck at. As Yuri left, Sam came over to let Neil know the pizza was ready.

"I figured you wouldn't want to leave this weird game, so I brought a piece for you," she said. "We should go soon, though. It's getting really late."

"Okay, thanks. I'll be done soon," said Neil, barely paying attention. With that, Sam went back to the table and Neil played on, following Wayoh off the farm to an ostrich racetrack. As they walked along paths illuminated by the setting sun, Neil took a bite of his pizza, forgetting for an instant that *fruit*, of all things, was on his slice.

"*Puphfffpplle!*" he said, but then he kept chewing. The fresh pineapple was sweet, adding a new and delicious flavor to the cheese and the sauce. Neil finished his slice quickly, just as Wayoh explained the rules of the race. Neil swallowed the last bite of pizza and wiped his hands clean on his pants.

Wayoh led him to a starting line nestled in the cove of a beach of tropical white sand and palm trees. At the sound of the bell, Neil and a few other ostriches set off. The controls took some getting used to, but Neil quickly got the hang of it. Neil won the first round and then kept on winning.

"Yes!" Neil whooped as he won another round. A few of the islanders in the restaurant began taking note, and a crowd started to form around him. Soon Neil found himself at the final race and even closer to beating the previous high score. His challenger was Ozzie Tritch, described by the game as "a real no-goodnik from the wrong side of Ostrich Town."

The start bell rang, and the ostriches bolted onto an open beach. Neil took the lead, his ostrich skimming over shallow water to sandbar checkpoints that rose out of the crystalline waves.

"This is awesome," Neil said, maneuvering the controls every which way. His attention was so focused on the screen that he didn't notice a group of burly guys coming into Penelope's all dressed in uniforms of black pants and muscle tees. They kept glancing behind them, as if waiting for the entrance of someone important.

A local kid who had been watching Neil's game broke from the circle and tapped Neil on the shoulder. "Listen, don't ask questions, but you should go. Harris is about to be here, and he'll want to play," he urged.

"But I've still got two lives! And I just got a talon upgrade!" Neil replied. He was racing toward an island where a tall waterfall flowed. The finish-line beacon flashed just behind it, and Neil knew the only way to win was to splash through to the other side. His tongue curled to the corner of his mouth in concentration.

Ignoring the kid, Neil had his ostrich take three running strides, then jump through the falling water and over black volcanic rock. Flowing lava peeked out from underneath cracks in the ground, and a pitch-black tunnel led to the level's finish line. But despite Neil's attempts to dissuade the other boy, he kept tapping on Neil's shoulder.

"Seriously," the boy insisted, his voice strained.

But then in walked a tall, gangly, pimply boy of no more than fourteen. His hair was wild and unruly, like he had just woken up. His left arm rested in a sling.

"You need to get out of here," said the local boy.

"Can't this guy wait until I'm done?" Neil turned to see the scared expression on the boy's face. "Um, okay," Neil said, feeling a little nervous. He ended the game and typed his name in all caps into the high-score slot, just beating the previous score-holder, who also held the other top eight spots. Then he turned and walked away, catching a glimpse of the newcomer—Harris, as the local had called him—staring him down from the corner. For a moment, their eyes locked. Neil shivered at the cold intensity of Harris's gaze before following the rest of his fellow recruits out the doorway.

CHAPTER

17

AS THE GROUP STARTED BACK TOWARD THE BARN, SAM lingered to walk with Neil. He trotted to catch up with her, and they set out together in the cricket-filled night.

"So, did you take top score, ostrich racer?" she said, nudging him.

"You know it," Neil replied. It was weird, talking to Sam and knowing that she knew all his secrets, including the time he accidentally wet his pants twice at the same science fair. But it was a good kind of weird, he thought. And the silence between them wasn't awkward.

The two walked together in step, gazing up at the stars that glistened like tiny holes in a fort's sheet cover.

"Nice—you can really see Cassiopeia without any light pollution," said Sam, her mouth barely open as her head leaned backward.

"Cassowhat?" Neil asked.

"Cassiopeia. Come on, you don't know what that is?"

"No. I only know like, a dipper. Maybe two," Neil confided. "I know there's something like a rabbit and twins and a lion that runs a zoo? Is that right?"

Sam burst out laughing and did a double take back at Neil.

"Are you serious? I can't believe you don't know them. I love constellations."

"Lemme guess—they're one of your seventeen favorite things?"

"Yeah," Sam said, but her tone faded into a bit of seriousness.

"Oh, um, sorry," Neil stammered, worried he'd said something wrong. "I think it's cool that you have seventeen. I didn't mean anything by that." The barn slowly appeared in the distance, and the waves of Jones's snoring rippled out over the coarse grass.

"No, it's not that," Sam replied, back from whatever thought she'd been temporarily lost in. "Just . . . growing up and moving a lot, I liked knowing that something stayed the same." Neil nodded. "Okay. So that, there? That's Ursa Major. It's pretty big. You should be able to remember that. See how it looks like a bear?" She pointed, and Neil squinted an eye to follow.

"Totally," he fibbed. But he repeated the name in his head three times, just to make sure it stuck. He looked down to see the ancient barn's outline as they caught up with everyone else.

Carefully peeling back the same loose slat of the barn as before, Neil held it open as the others began to crawl in silently.

Once everyone was back inside, Neil replaced the slat and made his way to his noisy sleeping bag. Adrenaline was still coursing through him, making him feel wide-awake. A hypnotic bongo drum and an ostrich race looped in his brain, but somehow, eventually, his eyes closed for the night.

★ ★ ★

A second passed—or what seemed like a second—before Jones was above Neil's face, shaking him awake.

"Rise and shine!" Jones said. "Change of plans." He was in full SEAL-grade stealth scuba gear, as were Wells and Lopez behind him. They wore black wet suits and sleek backpacks for tanks and supplies, as well as comically large flippers.

"You're looking spry today, Jonesy," said Biggs. "If I may call you Jonesy."

"It's Major Jones, sir."

"Sir, yes, sir, Major Grumpy Gus."

Neil looked down at his military-issued watch, which read 0427 hours. His eyes had been shut for only a few hours, but they stung so much it felt like even less.

"Soldiers, get ready," Jones announced. "Going off our previous recon, we found the heat signatures of our men. They're being held captive on the island connected to this by a suspension bridge, inside an old warehouse."

I knew it!

"While we can't be certain, we're assuming, as we thought before, that's where we'll find our plane as well." Jones stood over the still-sleepy recruits in front of him and tossed around packs of MREs to a chorus of groans. After all, everyone had just eaten pizza mere hours before.

"We've been able to get diagnostics on their

warehouse, and we've found a weakened entry point," Jones continued. "It's on the northwest side, only accessible from the shoreline."

"What about that grid preventing our communication? Have we done anything to fix that?" JP asked.

"It is what it is, kid, and there's nothing we can do to fix it. We tried unplugging everything we have, then plugging it back in, and nothing worked. We're on our own for this one."

"Really? Because if I could just try to take a look, I'm pretty sure—"

"Listen, kid," the major cut in. "We don't have time for whatever thing you learned at computer camp. It's time for action. Now, pay attention, because I'm only saying this once." Jones's eyes were lit up with a feverish excitement, just the way he'd looked earlier at the Decider. "The mission should go as planned. None of you will leave your assigned Chameleon. You fly us there; we secure our soldiers, find the missing fighter, and head back to the USS *Martin Van Buren*. Got it?"

Neil noticed how confident in the plan Jones seemed, glossing over things like how to break into a protected warehouse and find an aircraft that was specifically designed to be untraceable to the human eye. But Jones just kept on explaining, highlighting the fence outlining the perimeter of the warehouse.

"This chain-link fence covers up the remains of an old shipping dock," the major said. "From the looks of it, it was completed only recently, and not very well. There's a small gap between the fence and the ocean's floor—this will be our point of entry."

"You're gonna dive down there?" questioned Trevor.

"You better believe it, Grunsten. Me, Wells, and Lopez here could dive two hundred meters without a tank if we had to," Jones said.

"Hey, you guys be careful. I'm afraid of the bends, and I've never even done scuba," warned Biggs.

"Moonbeam, seal it. You will drop us off at an old shipping buoy offshore. Just inside the entrance to the complex there's a grassy courtyard, maybe the size of half a football field. You will proceed there and wait in the camouflage-activated Chameleons. We'll go in, do our thing, get out, and pile in with our men."

"What's the mission's name?" asked Waffles, who was the first one ready for action, already applying camouflage face paint. Most likely unnecessary face paint.

"Name? This is search-and-rescue file number nine-eight-four-six. That's the only name this thing will have," Jones said, shrugging off Waffles's question.

"What? This thing's gotta have some sizzle! You're telling me we're rolling in there without something awesome to call it, like Operation Hush-Up Scoop Job! Or Falcon Swoop Infinity?" Waffles exclaimed. "Those are just ideas, of course. We're just brainstorming here. But something, right?"

"Kid, this isn't a mission that gets a name. The only thing we're calling it is late, since their guards are switching duty soon," Jones replied. "Now, man your jets!"

He threw open the barn doors, and everyone scrambled into their fighters, Waffles still mumbling possible mission names. The pilots fired up the engines immediately and strapped themselves in, preparing to fly the most advanced fighters in history on a few hours of sleep.

The three fighter jets took off and began circling the outline of the island. It was early morning, and the sun cast a foggy yellow glow over the islands while the Chameleons broadcast a perfect re-creation of the surrounding sky.

The planes flew close enough for the recruits to see the warehouse, its tall concrete walls and spiraling barbed wire half covered in morning fog. On his mark, Jones signaled for the cockpit doors of each fighter to open, and the three scuba-gear-clad soldiers checked their helmets and dropped backward, completing a full rotation before hitting the water.

Neil watched them sink into the waves below, making their way to the barricaded back entrance of the giant warehouse, where waves splashed loudly against the concrete walls and over giant square boulders covered in algae.

Trevor flew lead in formation, directing the others to the large, grassy courtyard that Jones had described. The jets moved stealthily, careful to land as quietly as possible. Guards stood at each corner of the large enclosure and another at a tower above the compound's front entrance. None of them noticed as the landing gear for each invisible Chameleon made soft contact with the ground below.

CHAPTER 18

THE RECRUITS SAT IN A SLEEPY FOG OF SILENCE IN THE invisible fighters, watching the guards pace back and forth on patrol, carrying extremely thin baseball bats. The guards were all in uniform, wearing khaki pants, brown boots, sunglasses, and short-sleeved button-down shirts with a blue-and-yellow patch on the right sleeve. Neil strained his eyes to examine the patches, which looked like blue circles with some kind of picture inside, but he couldn't make out the details. He rubbed his eyes, still feeling the sting of their exhaustion. Late-night gaming sessions had put him in this state before, but he had always had the promise of eight hours of sleep in flannel sheets ahead of him. Now he struggled to keep his head from bobbing like a marionette's.

Around them, the giant concrete warehouse was completely sealed in, with tall fencing and loops of razor wire along the guards' pathway on top. Only the highest floor of the building was lined in windows of black-tinted glass. Neil had played enough Super Chopper: Revenge of the Rotor Man to notice what looked to be a helipad on the roof. To the side, behind giant sliding metal gates, was a gravelly driveway that ended in a loop. Two rugged jeeps and a glistening convertible sat parked at the end.

What could need all this protection? Neil wondered, drifting in and out of consciousness.

He was just starting to nod forward when one guard, walking on the top of the building, seemed to flicker and disappear. Neil pushed his fists into his eyes and rubbed them.

"Whoa, Trevor, are you getting this?" Neil asked. "Did you see that person just disappear?"

Trevor looked at Neil like he was starting to lose it. "If you mean that guy right there, then no, he didn't disappear," Trevor said. "Are you even looking in the right direction?"

Neil shrugged. With the amount of sleep he'd had over the last two nights, he thought he was probably hallucinating.

His eyes started to drift closed again, so he pinched himself to stay awake. Suddenly, the exterior doors leading into the courtyard opened.

"We've got movement on the outside doors," Neil radioed. He watched as what looked to be the two captured pilots were escorted out into the shaggy green grass, blindfolds securely in place. Three hulking guards in matching khaki were behind them.

Neil blinked furiously, rubbing the sleep from his eyes, and surveyed the scene. He watched as the heavy door closed behind them and other guards moved past on their rounds. What had happened to Jones, Lopez, and Wells?

After quickly doing a guard head count, Neil saw an opportunity.

"Sam, read me?" Neil asked.

"Copy that, ManofNeil. Those our men?" she asked.

"They are. Listen, I have an idea. We don't know

how much longer Jones and the others will be in there. But our pilots are *here*, with only three guards. We outnumber these guys four to one."

"That leaves just one human limb for each of us to restrain. I'd say that's pretty doable," Sam replied.

"Everybody else? This could be our chance to make a move. What do you think?" Neil asked his fellow drowsy soldiers.

"We're probably not going to get much better odds than that," calculated JP. "I agree it's our best shot." A few others murmured in support.

"Are you kidding me?" Trevor snapped. "Look at them. They are guards! Let me remind you that *I'm* the only one who conquered the Decider."

Neil clenched his teeth. The only reason Trevor had "conquered" anything was because he'd stepped on Neil's face in the process.

"Let's vote on it," Sam suggested before Neil could say another word.

"Fine," Trevor snapped. "We can vote." But after the count, only two others voted with him: Yuri and Riley. Everyone else sided with Neil.

"Okay," Neil said. "That's a majority. Everybody,

follow my mark. Let's finish this mission before Jones even has to worry about it."

Following his lead, the kids all scrambled out of their fighters, opening the invisible cockpits and jumping outside.

"*Now!*" Neil yelled. They made a run for the three guards holding their pilots captive, shouting war cries as they each made for a limb.

Neil grabbed hold of a leg that felt like a small, strong sapling. He wrapped himself firmly around the guard's ankle and twisted until he felt the towering person beginning to fall toward the ground, his movement restricted.

Seeing the others springing to action, Yuri and Riley left the company of Trevor's scowl and sprinted awkwardly toward the commotion.

"Neil!" yelled Jason 1, who chucked his flight helmet like a football toward the guard Neil was trying to take down. It struck the guard's head with just enough force to send him barreling to the ground. "Touchdown!" Jason 1 turned and rushed to the aid of Jason 2.

Neil looked over at his victim—only to lock eyes with Jones.

"Andertol, what are you doing? You're blowing our cover!" shouted Jones, tearing off his sunglasses and stolen hat. He and the others had worn them to blend in, Neil realized. His hat had the same patch as the one on the sleeves of each guard.

What had he done? Jones, Wells, and Lopez had stolen uniforms, posing as guards, and had almost escaped with the captured pilots. Thinking he was helping— thinking he was doing something right—Neil had ruined everything.

"Stop, everyone, stop! Same team! Same team!" Neil screamed. He looked over to see that his plan, unfortunately, had worked. Wells and Lopez were on the ground, the laces of their boots tied securely to opposite wrists. It seemed Dale knew a thing or two about hog-tying wild animals.

Neil fumbled to untie Wells and Lopez so that they could all escape, but it was too late—the real guards were running their way. A siren started to blare angrily through the courtyard.

"Just go!" yelled Jones, yanking Neil up from where he knelt, still struggling with Dale's complicated knots. "There's no time. I'll hold them off. Just don't let them get the Chameleons!"

"But we can't leave—

"Yes, you can!" Jones bellowed, giving Neil a shove. Then he turned to face the two guards attacking him. "You want some of this?" he growled. "I could take out you scrawny punks with my eyes closed!"

"Come on!" Neil said, directing the rest of the recruits to follow him. He was running faster than he'd ever run in his life, faster than he even thought was possible. But not all the kids were so lucky. Next to him, Corinne was yanked back by one of the hulking guards. Another snatched up Riley, who started thrashing as he was lifted into the air like a potted plant. Neil hesitated for an instant. How could he let his friends be captured?

"Run, my lordship! Save thyself!" crowed Riley.

Neil turned and sprinted with the others back toward the planes. There were a few collisions, as the Chameleons were still invisible, but using the hand sensor technology, the rest of the recruits found their way inside the planes.

★ ★ ★

From the cockpits the kids watched the chaos unfolding on the lawn. Jones was being attacked by five or six guards. Four each were needed for both Wells and Lopez. And a few more of their own had been captured—Yuri and the Jasons as well as Corinne and Riley.

"Time for takeoff," Sam said from her jet.

Trevor, who was back in the pilot's seat, turned on the ignition, and they lifted off. The plane quickly started to move up and away from the courtyard. Next to Trevor, Neil pressed his face against the window to try to get a good view of what was happening. A flurry of guards ran out of the warehouse, followed by another person who seemed to be in charge—he wore a white captain's hat that reminded Neil of Weo's, but Neil couldn't see much else.

Come on, look up, look up, Neil thought furiously. This was the person who'd stolen a Chameleon and now had captured his friends. He had to see who it was.

As Neil was about to turn away back to his copiloting duties, the person with the hat tilted his head up. Neil gasped aloud. It was *Harris*, the kid from the pizza place the night before. And he was looking straight at them.

CHAPTER

19

THE CHAMELEONS DARTED BACK THE WAY THEY HAD COME, the nervous pilots frantically guiding them to the main island. A few minutes later, the three planes landed at the barn, and everyone immediately climbed out of the fighters. The remaining recruits all began to talk at once, yelling over one another, but Neil remained silent. This was his fault, and he knew that only he could get his friends back. He turned around slowly, surveying who was left: Trevor, Sam, Biggs, JP, and the twins, Dale and Waffles.

- -

"Well, what do we do now?" demanded Trevor of no one in particular.

"Yeah, what now?" repeated Waffles, who was probably in desperate need of a multiplayer game, or something with high-fructose corn syrup.

"This was your big idea, Ashley! It's all your fault we're in this mess!" Trevor reminded Neil.

"Dudes, chill. Please!" Biggs shouted.

"What do we do without Jones? What are they gonna do with everybody else?" shouted Dale.

"Everyone, just *shut up*!" Sam stood at the center of the group, her chest heaving in frustration. She grabbed Biggs's hacky sack from the ground. Biggs started to open his mouth in protest, but she glared at him, staring him down. "Now," she said more calmly, "if you have an idea, please tell the group, one at a time. You can only talk if you have the hacky sack. Okay?"

Waffles reached to yank the beanbag out of her grip. "I say we just storm the fences, plow in there, and rescue everyone," he said. "We've got three of the most advanced fighters ever! Why are we just sitting around waiting?"

"Because that's a great way to get killed," said Trevor,

pulling the hacky sack from Waffles. "What if, instead, we find a way to disable their communications grid?"

"And how are we supposed to do that?" Waffles shot back.

"No talking without the sack!" Sam interrupted. JP took the hacky sack swiftly and held it close to his chest, refusing to surrender it to Trevor. "Well, Jones said there was a distress signal or something, right? A magnetic pulse? Could we set that off from the planes we have?"

Sam held out her hand for the hacky sack, shaking her head. "I don't know if we could figure that out without actually destroying one of the planes. I'm pretty sure that's a last-minute distress-call type of thing. Like if it's really under attack."

The group fell silent. No one had any idea what to do.

"Tell you what—I think we just need some food," Biggs said suddenly. "Let's go back to the pizza place, see if Penny is setting up for breakfast. Maybe we can figure something out there."

Tired and without any better ideas, everyone mumbled in agreement. They followed Biggs out of the barn, hustling along the path they'd walked just a few hours ago. The sun was rising on the horizon, illuminating everything with a pale-gold light. A few surfers waded in the water, their dark shadows bobbing with the current.

"What are we gonna do, Neil?" Sam whispered, falling into step beside him.

"I don't know." Neil sighed. He knew it sounded crazy, but he really wanted to tell Sam what he'd seen earlier. "Listen," he said, "remember that kid from last night? Harris, the one from that pizza place?"

"Yeah, what about him?" Sam asked. She kicked a small rock with the toe of her shoe, moving it forward along the dirt path, only to kick it again in a few steps.

"Well, I think he's behind this," Neil blurted out.

Sam paused in her tracks. "Okay," she said carefully. "What makes you say that?"

"Let me start over. When we were coming in yesterday, we kinda crashed on the smaller island."

"You *what?*"

"It was totally Trevor's fault. I mean, we were fine, but we lost our gear in the jungle and . . ."

"Whoa, slow down, partner. Jungle?"

"Sorry," he said. "Yeah, we took the scenic way in.

Anyway, Jones made me and Trevor go find the gear, and we wound up meeting this kid, Weo, who lives in a tree house."

"Oh . . . that's cool," said Sam, who seemed a little shocked by all this.

"Yeah. Well, sort of. He told us about the islands and how there was this scary billionaire who lived on his own island," Neil continued. "And that fortress or what-ever we were just in—that's where the billionaire lives or works or something."

"But what makes you think this has anything to do with Harris?" Sam asked.

"Just now, when we were at the warehouse and Jones and everyone got caught, I saw him," Neil insisted. "And all the guards were definitely following his orders. You could tell by the way they were answering to him."

Sam frowned, considering what Neil had just told her. "It's possible," she said. "At the very least, he's con-nected to the bad guy."

Neil and Sam kept walking, falling silent as they both thought through possible plans.

"You know, I remember how weird everybody got when he came into Penny's last night. Something about that didn't seem right," she said as they approached the entrance of the pizza place.

The front door was locked, but Neil could hear Penny humming as she flipped an omelet in a frying pan behind the counter. "Excuse me, Penny?" he yelled, leaning on the door and cupping his hands around his mouth. Moments later, the door opened to reveal Penny standing there, grinning and holding a giant mixing bowl.

"Well, look who's up bright and early," she said. "It's Mr. Picky Eater and his friends. I'm happy to whip you kids up some omelets, as long as you aren't as picky as Plain Cheese over here." Everyone quickly stammered to assure her they weren't picky at all. "Great," Penny said. "In that case, get ready for the best ostrich-egg omelet you've ever tasted."

"The only ostrich-egg omelet we've ever tasted," Neil muttered.

"I heard you," Penny said. "And that changes today. Sit down, kids."

They all plopped down at one of the long tables and leaned back, too exhausted even to talk, while Penny started frying their omelets on the grill. A few minutes later, a haggard group walked into the restaurant. They all wore polo shirts that said, in dark cursive, FIVE-PIECE BANDWIDTH TECH SUPPORT.

"Hello, computer boys," said Penny. They all waved. "Late night at the fire jam?"

"Ugh, you don't even know. I think I woke up with two dozen glow sticks around my body," said one of them.

"Still not ready for that Wi-Fi, Penny?" asked another. "We could have you up and running in no time. You could be selling your pizzas online! You're missing out on a big opportunity!"

She responded with a laugh. "The day this place is online is the day I quit making pizza," she said. "Anyway, you boys need to finish up tinkering with that video game here. Your toolbox is still behind it. When you unplug it, I swear the whole thing nearly sets fire."

"Soon, Penny. We're too tired to even move right now, but we promise. As long as it stays plugged in, you'll be fine."

Penny laughed and turned to the recruits, still wiped out at their table. "Kids, you know Five-Piece Bandwidth? The only tech support on the island! They sing harmonies while providing technical assistance," she announced like a proud aunt.

"Nice to meet you," Neil mumbled, and the tech support guys nodded back.

"Neil," said Sam, leaning in and lowering her voice. "Tell everybody what you think you saw."

And so Neil told the other recruits his theory about the mysterious billionaire who'd captured the Chameleon and how he thought that billionaire was Harris. He was worried no one would believe him, but they were glued to his words. "So, yeah," he concluded. "I can't really say for certain, but I know I saw him lead all those guards out, yelling at them. If he's not in charge, he's at least someone important."

"Okay," JP said thoughtfully. "If this Harris is the guy, how do we get to him?"

"Sam could go on a date with him!" Trevor exclaimed. "She could make him fall in love with her and then force him to tell us where everyone is held captive."

"Ew, gross," replied Sam. "No, for so many reasons. The first of which being what I imagine his breath smells like."

"Should we try breaking in?" offered Dale. "I could shoot a rope up to the top if we wanted to climb. I just turned pro in Rodeo Ricky Presents: Lads and Lassos."

"I don't know if that's enough to get past Harris's defenses," Neil said dubiously.

"You say Harris?" one of the uniformed tech support members cut in on his way back from the counter. He was large, with chubby cheeks and parted greasy hair, and he looked sort of like a sumo wrestler in training. He blew on a pineapple pizza to cool it down, then looked up at them. "That little punk owes us a thousand bucks. If you see him, make sure to give him a piece of my mind."

"All our minds," added another of the tech support team. He took a bite of his pizza, chewing with his mouth open.

"We rigged his warehouse into a hashtag paradise," said another member, stuffing his mouth full of melted cheese.

"And I still have this piece-of-junk arcade game he gave me," Penny joined in, shouting over the sizzle of ostrich-egg omelets in a saucepan. "I wish you would just tell him to come pick it up. Some moneymaker that was. What person comes to play around with little ostriches?"

Neil felt a little bad—he'd thought the game was kind of fun.

"Hey, guys," Sam said, in a way that Neil recognized from all their games together. It meant she was coming up with a plan. "If we can't break in . . . we should just get *invited* in."

Everyone looked at her, slightly unsure. Penny rang a silver bell, announcing that their ostrich-egg omelets were ready and waiting.

"What's the one thing no nerd can live without?" Sam asked as a smile stretched across her face.

CHAPTER 20

MINUTES LATER, SAM, NEIL, TREVOR, AND BIGGS appeared from the back room of Penny's, all of them dressed in the uniforms graciously on loan from the Five-Piece Bandwidth team. They each wore a floppy mesh hat, too-large polo shirt, and baggy black cargo pants.

Neil pulled at the collar of the humongous shirt. He had a flashback to shopping with his mother, when he would walk out of the department-store dressing room wearing an outfit two sizes too big, and she would loudly reassure him—and everyone in the store—that he would "grow into it." Sometimes Neil still woke up in the middle of the night in a cold sweat, signs for the Junior Men's section burning marks into his brain.

"This just might work," said one of the tech nerds, standing in his white undershirt and music-note-patterned boxer shorts. "They've never really looked us in the eye there, so I don't think they'll notice any difference. We should just make sure we teach you our latest song. It's sort of a razzle-dazzle piece loosely based on defragmenting a hard drive."

"Oh," Neil said. "Sorry, but I don't really sing." Sometimes he sang Miley Cyrus in the shower, but no one needed to know that.

The tech guys all looked at him as if he'd just asked them what YouTube was. "Dude, that's our thing. You *have* to sing. Otherwise, he'll know you're total fakes. Our singing really sets him off. It engages the customer."

"It's okay, I got it," Biggs cut in. "I don't want to brag, but I did make it through one round of untelevised cuts on last season's *Sing the Songs of Others: America's Talent.* You can just harmonize off of me, Neil."

"Thanks," Neil said. Knowing Biggs, though, his song would be about something like the many alternate ways to capture rainwater. He turned to JP. "JP, are you sure you can take down the wireless?" They had to disable Harris's system first so that he'd call the local tech support in.

"Easy," JP assured him. "I'll take a Chameleon and head over to the warehouse's electrical outpost. I saw it when we were there earlier. Everything technical and electrical seems to be run out of it."

"Where was it?" asked Sam.

"It was just outside that courtyard, a small box sticking up from the bushes past the northwest corner. I'm thinking if we can knock out whatever's blocking our transmissions back to the base, we can get air support to come help us in no time. I'll just need a few minutes. First I can take out their internet so that he calls you in. And then, if you can buy me a few more seconds, I'll try to take down that grid or whatever they have blocking us."

"You think you can do all that?" Neil asked.

"Please. I could've done all that three years ago. This thing is going to be one giant hot spot by the time I'm finished," JP replied. "You'll be able to get a signal on the moon if you want. So who's coming with me?"

– –

"I'll go with you, JP," Trevor said, seeming eager to leave the rest of the group.

"Wait," a tall member of the tech support said. His voice was a gravelly baritone, perfect for singing slow jams and binary beats. "I hate to break it to you, but they might notice if one of the guys is a girl, seeing as how they do *sort of* know us."

"But my hair is up," Sam protested, pointing to where her hair was pulled up into a bun under her cap.

"You still look girlie," the tech guy said—cautiously, as though worried he was being offensive.

"Fine," Sam said, taking off the cap and tossing it to Trevor. She grinned. "Hope that sweet falsetto of yours is ready, Grunsten."

"Just don't crash the getaway plane, Samantha," Trevor replied.

It was agreed that Sam would fly JP to circle the warehouse while he took out the internet connection. Then she would land in the courtyard and wait for Neil and the others to appear with the missing pilots and the rest of their team. As soon as Harris called for help with the internet, Trevor, Biggs, and Neil would enter, posing as the tech support.

"What should we do?" asked Dale. "We could ride along with somebody."

"Actually," Sam thought aloud, "we may need a little bit of a distraction. Anything you guys can do to take care of the guards, keep their focus away so that when we escape, they won't have time to react?"

Waffles smiled brightly. "Distraction is my middle name," he said.

"Your middle name is Gary," Dale corrected. "But, yeah, we're good at distractions. We've got that covered."

Now that everyone knew their roles in the mission, they each ate a few more bites of omelet, then set out. JP and Sam went back to the barn to fly one of the Chameleons, while Neil and the others stayed put to determine the best distraction for the patrolling guards.

Sure enough, minutes later, a call was placed to Five-Piece Bandwidth tech support. The tallest tech support geek handed the phone to Biggs with a nod.

"Five-Piece Bandwidth tech support," Biggs said. "How can I help you, or how can you help me? Or rather, how can we help the universe help each other?"

Neil made a slicing motion at his neck for Biggs to

pull it back—he only had one simple job, and he was somehow Biggs-ing it up.

"Okay, right on. Sounds like a classic case of web leprosy," Biggs said, nodding as if giving an official doctor's diagnosis. "We'll send a crew to come check it out in a few. We'll ring the doorbell at the entrance."

Biggs kept nodding, listening to what Neil assumed were instructions on how to get in. "No problem. We'll be at the entrance in ten minutes," Biggs said, winking and pumping his fist. "Goood byiyiyiyiii . . . ," Biggs sang, trailing off.

"Okay, this guy is definitely in charge of singing," one of the tech support nerds said, pointing at Biggs.

"Thanks," Biggs said, blushing. "But just so you all know, I may have to start singing in my head voice once we get into some of the—"

"All right, team," Neil said, cutting off Biggs. "You're all clear on your jobs, right?" He could see the glassy stare of nervousness reflected in their eyes. *What would Jones say?* he wondered.

"Recruits, I think this is what Jones was telling us about," Neil started in a faltering tone. "We're—I'm—scared, and alone. But we've got each other. And the rest of our team needs us. We can do this!" Everyone looked at one another in silence for a moment.

"Nice, Neil. I sort of want to start a slow clap for you," Biggs said, impressed.

"Wait, but we need a name!" Waffles exclaimed.

"Dude, I'm not sure we've got ti—"

"No way. We're doomed if we don't have the perfect name for this mission." Waffles paused for a long second, looking into the distance as though fondly remembering game names from times past.

"I've got it: Operation Howling Lone Wolves," he said with confidence.

"Eh, let's keep trying," Dale said. "Isn't it bad grammar to pluralize a lone something, anyway?"

"Okay, maybe not my best. I'll keep at it," Waffles called after the others.

★ ★ ★

The Five-Piece Bandwidth car was a cherry-red jeep, with the name of the group stenciled on the driver's-side door. Neil was behind the wheel, as it had been decided that driving duty would go to the person with the highest score on Six-Point Turn: Johnny Diesel's Driver's Ed.

"Okay," JP said, radioing them from the Chameleon,

which Sam was landing in the courtyard. "Internet's down. So once you're in, you'll . . . ," he prompted.

"Let them know that we need to take down the power for a bit," Neil answered from the driver's seat.

"Right. If their lock system is electronic, which I'm guessing it is, cutting out the power should disable the locks—so you can hopefully free our guys from wherever they're being held."

"Okay," Neil said, and started the engine, gripping the steering wheel tight.

"You've got this, Neil!" Sam encouraged. "It's all about your attitude. When you get to the gates, just drive right through. You've done it dozens of times before—well, virtually."

Neil nodded and moved the gearshift to *R*. "Ready!" he exclaimed. The car lurched backward, and he quickly slammed on the brake. "I mean, reverse. Of course. Just making sure everybody's on their toes."

Trevor and Biggs glanced down to make sure their seat belts were on tight.

CHAPTER

21

SMALL ROCKS AND GRAVEL POPPED UNDER THE TREADS of the jeep as Neil drove forward—very, very slowly, with his right foot on the gas pedal and his left on the brake. The road he was on made a large loop around the remnants of the bonfire and funneled toward a rickety floating bridge connecting Brosiah Bay to Harris's island.

"Nice and easy," advised Biggs from the passenger seat.

Trevor sat in the back, nervously bending the brim

of his new hat. Their vehicle crawled out over the connecting bridge, which sank lower into the water from the weight of their car. Neil turned the wheel left and right, constantly making adjustments as if he were in a video game. Finally, he cleared the bridge, and their jeep's wheels clawed up the rocky incline at the threshold of the warehouse. At the gate, Neil slammed on the brake with both feet, tightening everyone's seat belts in the process.

"Jeez, Ashley. Easy on the whiplash."

The doors ahead were maybe twenty feet high, and they opened into the base like a centuries-old castle wall. Neil rolled the jeep up the driveway and parked behind a battered Humvee and the glossy convertible Neil had seen earlier.

He jammed the gearshift forward to *P* then cautiously lifted his foot from the brake pedal. *Whew.* The sounds of flying seagulls and waves crashing against rocks floated through the half-open windows.

They all crept out of the car and looked up at the concrete monstrosity in front of them. The sun danced off the tinted glass at its top. Two giant stainless-steel doors marked the gateway to whatever lurked inside, and a camera turned a cold, metallic eye toward them from each corner. Neil gulped and started to walk as confidently as he could, Biggs and Trevor following behind.

Neil reached the doorway and wrapped his clammy hand around the sun-warmed handle. His hands vibrated with nerves, his mind reviewing and re-reviewing the haphazard plan they'd hatched only minutes before. "Okay," he said in a voice just above a whisper. "Let's go rescue our friends."

The group rang the doorbell, and when a buzz released the lock, they pushed forward into the dark foyer, pausing for a second to get acclimated. The door slammed shut behind them, and they all jumped in surprise.

As Neil's eyes adjusted, he looked down the hallway. It was cold and drab, the concrete floor etched with a logo—the same logo that he'd seen earlier on the sleeves of the guards. It was an ostrich, its head forward and wings back as it sprinted ahead. Feather Duster, the video game at Penny's! That was where the logo was from. *But why is it all over everything?*

At the end of the corridor were two swinging metal doors, and on either side were doors with clear-glass windows revealing rooms full of empty desks and aged cardboard storage boxes. One of the office lights was turned on, the fluorescent bulb flickering overhead. Neil crept slowly toward it to look inside.

The first thing he saw was a poster for Feather Duster and a huge bulletin board crammed with dozens of magazine and newspaper clippings. While some of the print was too fine to read, the ones that stuck out to Neil said things like "worst game of the year," "a must-not-play," and "controls so unbelievably unintuitive, you'd think a real ostrich created this monstrosity." At the center of the room was a barren desk that played host to scattered pens and paper clips, as well as a name tag with VICE PRESIDENT etched into white plastic.

"This must be the warehouse. Like, where they used to make the games," Trevor muttered, looking over Neil's shoulder.

"I think you're right," Neil agreed.

Behind Neil, something clattered loudly to the ground, and Neil and Trevor looked up sharply.

"Sorry," Biggs whispered, having knocked a plaque off the wall that read OSTRICH ACHIEVEMENT AWARD, FROM THE UNITED OSTRICH FARMERS ASSOCIATION.

Neil cringed, but no one came to examine the source of the noise. "Come on. Let's go."

The three fake technical assistants took quick, nervous steps toward the end of the hallway, glancing at the dented doors ahead. They reminded Neil of the doors in the deli of his grocery store, accustomed to fully packed dollies constantly bashing into them.

"It's like . . . it doesn't really *feel* like a bad guy's hideout," Biggs said, sounding a bit disappointed. "I know this sounds weird, but a small part of me wanted to see a cool underground training facility. With dudes just goin' nuts on some punching bags and stuff."

Neil, who had expected something similar, nodded. At last they reached the doors at the end of the hallway. With a deep breath, Biggs pushed them forward, and the hinges squeaked to announce their arrival.

Inside the warehouse itself, the ceiling was high, boasting exposed beams and silver scoops of floodlights. Forklifts sat dormant in the farthest corners of the room, with giant boxes filling most of the other space. They were stacked in uniform rows, and all had the Feather Duster logo inked onto their sides.

As they walked on, the room filled with the sound

of Harris's gritty, impatient screams, and he soon came into view. "I don't care how it gets done—just do it. The wire transfer happens at four p.m. sharp. If you can't do it, you'll be replaced with someone who can!" he shouted at a geeky-looking guard glued to a laptop. "You're easily replaceable."

At the sound of their footsteps, Harris looked up, noticing their arrival. "Good," he sighed. "The singing IT fools are here."

Neil tugged at the floppy mesh hat perched on his nest of shaggy hair. He averted his eyes with a whistle, glancing around all sides of the compound.

His whistling stopped, though, at the sight of a window-lined corner office labeled MANAGER ON DUTY. Two of the four walls of the office were glass, allowing the person in charge an unobstructed view of the warehouse floor.

Inside, the office looked much like the other abandoned workspaces they'd seen in the hallway outside—a desk littered with papers and framed pictures. One such photo, with a wooden frame, was a horizontal shot that showed two happy fathers hoisting smiling sons high on their shoulders. Their toothy grins were as white as the captain hats on their heads. But unlike the other offices, this one was full of people—Neil's friends.

Jones was strapped to the main chair behind the desk, looking extremely weathered and disheveled, his cheek somehow still full of sunflower seeds. He grimaced, and Neil realized that his hands were tied with a Feather Duster controller. From the looks of it, his punishment was being forced to play the now-extinct game.

The rest of the group—Wells and Lopez, as well as the two soldiers Neil assumed were the captured pilots, the Jasons, Yuri, Riley, and Corinne—were all tied to chairs, desks, and other office furniture. Two fat-faced guards stood outside, keeping watch, while a huge padlock secured the door.

Neil stared furiously into the room, but everyone was either fixated on Jones's score or the floor, their heads lolling with drowsiness. None of them met Neil's gaze, but Neil wished he could just run up and free them. While most of the guards were armed with nothing more than promotional ostrich claws—which Neil now remembered were from a failed fast-food promotion—those in charge of the prisoners held huge Taser-like pieces of equipment, specifically designed for larger animals. *Probably ostriches*, Neil thought. The gray-and-black weapons, whatever they were, hummed in a way that made Neil more than a little nervous.

"Are you waiting for an invitation?" Harris snapped. "The fiber optics are down. I need you to make them *not* down."

Neil cleared his throat and began looking through the bag of tools he'd lugged in. Biggs started to hum, slowly turning it into a made-up song. He sang it like the classic rock Neil remembered from family vacations at his uncle Chet's house.

"*We will haaave to shut down your eleeeeectric system,*" Biggs crooned.

"*Shut it down! Shut it down!*" sang Trevor, in a high-pitched opera voice.

Neil smiled. *I can't believe they're pulling this off. Do I try to just free-jazz a few lines here?*

"*Just for a one-ah-two, a one-to-ten min-utes,*" Biggs sang as his shoulders kept a rhythm.

"Yes, yes. That's fine. And you know the drill. Just keep that singing nonsense to yourselves. If I had any other options, believe me, I'd take them over having to listen to you all."

"So, what I think we'll have to do is shut down the whole electrical system for a minute or two. That'll give us enough time to hack into the firewall and reroute the encryption codes for the database wavelength programming. All standard stuff," Biggs made into a pseudo-song, clearly uncertain what he was saying.

Neil watched Harris grab a nearby goon. "So, are you going to turn off the electricity, or do I have to turn *you* off?"

"Do you need the electricity off for a while, or just a minute?" the guard asked Neil nervously. "Should I wait out there?"

"Ah, yeah, power outage should be no more than five minutes. We just want to start, ah, bootlegging the ZIP files so we can do a sweep on the connection," Neil said, his nerves causing him to spout any form of technical jargon he'd come across. He realized too late that he hadn't been singing.

Harris paused, his jaw clenched. "Wait, *say* that again," he demanded.

Neil grew nervous. He was not good at lying, or

singing, and his life now depended on him doing both.

But before he could even come up with a tune, he heard the thick outer doors of the main entrance open and abruptly close, just as they had when he and the others walked in. Neil began a long, deliberately phlegmy warm-up cough, hoping that whoever it was would distract Harris enough to make him forget his mistake.

"Penny's delivery. Have a large usual for you, Harris," said the voice of a pizza-delivery driver, his hands holding a piping-hot pineapple pie. He walked confidently onto the huge floor of the warehouse, like he'd obviously done many times before, and dropped off the box on a control console in the center of the giant room. Turning back around on his way out, he caught sight of Neil, and his face lit up. "Whoa, hey, man! Didn't see you there!" he exclaimed. "You killed that game last night. Look, I even got your haircut!" He lifted his black hat to reveal two missing patches of sideburn hair.

"Wait. Game? What game?" Harris asked, looking back and forth from the driver to Neil. "*My* game?"

"Yeah!" said the driver, who then remembered who

was asking. "I mean, yes, sir. Your game. He's the only one I've ever seen beat your score."

Harris turned to Neil with a growl. "ManofNeil. I've been waiting for you to show up again. Not just anybody comes in and beats my game."

"I didn't see your name on it," Neil replied.

"Oh, no? Should be on the back, near the *trademark*. I *invented* the game. It's mine. And now you are, too." He laughed. "Pretending to be part of Five-Piece Bandwidth? You should have stuck to gaming. At least that one can carry a tune," he added, nodding to Biggs.

"Thanks, man," Biggs said.

"Security!" Harris yelled, provoking a dozen khaki-sporting guards to burst out from every direction, dashing at Neil, Trevor, and Biggs.

"*Wait, what are you doooooooing?*" Biggs sang, somehow trying to keep the charade alive, or maybe just unable to stop singing. But Harris's men quickly had him tied up, squirming in their arms.

A guard unlocked the giant padlock on the manager's office door and shoved the three boys inside. Neil, Biggs, and Trevor were put in chairs and lashed down just like the others, their feet and legs restrained by zip ties and industrial-strength plastic wrap.

"No talking!" barked one of the guards—and no one argued, as the Taser over his shoulder probably had enough power to electrify a zoo.

Harris, flanked by a crew of his men, slammed the door shut and trudged toward the main entrance.

"They can't be alone. There were twelve of them at Penny's last night," he yelled. "Find the other four!"

Neil cringed as an alarm began to blast throughout the vast complex, but he couldn't move to put his hands over his ears. Wrenching in his chair, tightly wrapped into submission, Neil quickly looked around the office-turned-prison. A TV blared at high volume. It showed one of the earlier levels of Feather Duster.

I hope Sam and the others are okay, Neil thought. But he soon found out when all four of the remaining rescue-mission pilots—Sam, JP, Waffles, and Dale—were tossed into the office, too.

For some reason, Waffles and Dale were covered in multicolored body paint, with feathers sticking to them at various angles. They wore Halloween promotional ostrich hats that Neil had seen at the fire jam the night before.

"Found these two causing a scene, trying to act like ostriches out front," said the guard who escorted the twins into the holding cell.

"Sorry, guys," Waffles whispered. "Looks like Operation: Ostrich Freedom didn't go as well as we'd hoped."

CHAPTER

22

"WAIT!" NEIL CRIED OUT AFTER THE DEPARTING GUARDS. HE banged his head on the glass wall, and everyone got a little grossed out, as a night without a shower meant he left a greasy approximation of his forehead on the glass. But with his hands tied, he figured it was the next best thing.

"I want to speak to Harris!"

"It's no use, Neil. We've already tried the 'yelling for hours' approach," said Corinne.

Neil looked around the room—Jones, Wells, and Lopez had been stripped of their gear, their mouths duct-taped shut. The two captured pilots looked hungry and nearly on the brink of ostrich-racing-induced insanity.

Neil felt horrible. It was his fault this whole plan had backfired—if that pizza-delivery boy hadn't recognized him, if he hadn't insisted on playing Feather Duster through the final level last night, this wouldn't have happened. His mind raced to create a plan for escape.

"Well, look at it this way. At least now we have more contestants in our Feather Duster tournament," said Jason 1.

That's it! Neil thought. The only name holding the top scores belonged to Harris. That was the real reason Neil was locked up in a factory manager's office. And hopefully, it would be the reason he got out.

Neil squirmed to look at his watch. It was just past one p.m. Harris had said some kind of transfer would happen at four p.m. sharp. Whatever that was, Neil had a feeling it wasn't good.

"Hey!" Neil yelled again, trying to get the guards' attention.

"Quiet, my friend," urged Yuri. "Or else they'll make you be quiet."

"Hey! I want to talk to Harris! I want to speak to the guy in charge here!"

One of Harris's guards walked into the room, and Neil hurried to start talking before the guy could get Taser happy. "You tell Harris that if he wants to know the location of three more Chameleons on these islands, he has to come in here and talk to me," Neil said calmly. Behind his duct tape, Jones started mumbling something that made Neil a little glad he couldn't talk right now.

The guard conferred with his accomplice and left.

"I hope you know what you're doing, Neil," Sam warned, her complexion pale.

"I do," Neil said. He just hoped he was right.

★ ★ ★

An hour later, the guards returned from the front hallway with Harris in tow. Harris stepped into the prison and examined Neil with his cold, brown-flecked eyes, saying nothing. His one arm was still in a sling.

"Three more Chameleons?" he said finally.

"Yup. And if you want them, I can tell you where they are," Neil said. "But you have to beat me at Feather Duster. And claim your top spot back. Otherwise, no deal."

"You do know I *made* that game, right? I don't care about a stupid score on one stupid console. I have a million copies, and I've mastered every one. I know every detail of every level. I spent years inventing it."

Neil knew this wouldn't be easy.

"Who cares?" Neil said. "The one at Penny's—the only one on the island, the one everyone here plays—you know that's the only one that matters. If you don't accept my challenge, everyone will always know who *really* has the top score. So, what do you say? One-on-one, your game, your island, your record. I lose, you keep us locked up and get three more planes. You lose, you have to let us all go. Agreed?"

Neil was trying to act casual, but his stomach was twisting into knots, and he felt a pins-and-needles tingling in the tips of his fingers. He hoped his hunch was right—that if Harris had already stolen one of the jets, he would jump at the chance to get his hands on three more.

"Well," Harris said, his voice cool but his eyes lighting up in excitement, "I suppose I've got time for a quick scrimmage." He nodded to the guards. "Bring him," he said, and turned to go.

One of the goons untied Neil from the chair and threw a burlap bag over his head, then tossed him over his shoulder like a bag of peat moss. "Okay, really?" Neil protested. "You guys do know that I know where I'm going, right?"

"Silence!" yelled the guard as he shoved him into the backseat of a vehicle. Neil felt a body slide into the seat next to him and assumed it was Harris.

Questions. I should be asking questions. Neil had seen enough superhero and action movies to know that if he could keep the villain talking, Harris might eventually reveal something that could hurt him, some kind of weakness.

"So, what did you mean when said you made that game?" Neil asked, his nose rubbing against the fibrous bag enveloping his face.

Only silence. Neil heard the vehicle's ignition turn over.

"Like, did you design the cover art?" he persisted.

"Ha. So simple, your little thoughts," Harris replied. "I created it. Without any help or assistance."

"Oh, so you, like, wrote all the code for it? Designed the levels and stuff?" Neil asked.

"Of course," Harris responded. "I've been coding my whole life. Feather Duster was just my first game."

"What happened? Why did it get canceled? Did you not want to make it anymore?" Neil tried to remember the TV psychiatrists his mother loved, the way they shot rapid-fire questions at people to try to trip them up. Then again, their issues had to do with hoarders and people addicted to eating household cleaning supplies.

"Oh, it wasn't my choice. My—" Harris stopped himself.

Neil remained silent. He got the sense that if he pressed Harris, Harris would never admit what he was about to say.

"Father. My father cut the funding, the fool."

His father canceled his own son's game?

"He read too many of those articles," Harris went on, his voice tense. "The reviewers trashed it. They thought the start was boring, that the racing wasn't lifelike enough, that the controls were clunky," Harris fumed. "Like they would know! We had promotions, toys, tie-ins with pet stores, everything. And the second game was even better than the first!" Harris slammed a fist into his passenger-side door. "But those without faith will soon see how wrong they were."

"Need help with things on the ostrich front?" Neil offered from behind the bag on his head. "I think I might know a guy who's a real top-notch dude for ostrich-related stuff."

"The controls are fine! Not that you would know," Harris scoffed. "Not that anyone would know what riding an ostrich is like. Ridiculous to compare something you can't even understand."

"But this guy, Weo. He'd be—"

"Wait, what did you say?" Harris snapped. "What name did you just say?"

Neil felt that somehow he'd hit a nerve and wasn't sure if it was best to repeat it.

"Theo. My friend Theo? His family lives on a llama farm. He has a few ostriches he likes to keep around, too. For, ya know, getting groceries and stuff. The basics," Neil babbled on. "I could set you guys up with a chat thing, just to see if you're feeling good about—"

"You talk too much."

Seconds of silence stretched out, making their presence felt between the two boys, who both badly needed some sort of shampoo or conditioner or, at the very least, a bar of soap.

"What I don't understand," Neil tried again, "is what you want with the Chameleon. I mean, obviously it's insanely cool. You've flown it, right?" Silence. Neil blinked, wishing he could see Harris's expression, but he couldn't see anything through the weave of the burlap sack. "What I mean is, what's the connection between the Chameleon and Feather Duster? 'Cause if you're trying to make a game based on the Chameleon, it already exists. And now you've stolen a jet fighter from the military. Don't you know what kind of trouble you're about to be in?"

"Trouble?" Harris said, ignoring the rest of Neil's questions. "Trust me, you haven't seen anything close to trouble yet." Harris laughed madly, a menacing cackle of a laugh.

If this kid invented a video game, he can't be evil . . . can he?

"I noticed your arm was in a sling. How'd you hurt it?" Neil asked.

"Why do you care? It won't hinder my gaming, if that's what you're curious about," Harris said.

"Did you fall? As in, from high up?"

"No," Harris said quickly—too quickly. Neil knew he was getting to him.

"You fell from a net, didn't you?"

"No more questions."

The rough burlap could not contain the smile that was spreading over Neil's face.

★ ★ ★

As Neil felt the prod of a guard behind him, the burlap sack was ripped from his head, scratching his lips and eyelids. Another guard clipped the ties from his wrists. Neil stretched out his arms, which had been cramped up for hours, and flexed his fingers, ready to play.

They were standing in front of the Feather Duster game at Penny's place, and Neil watched Harris enter a code to skip the first few levels and go right to the race. Neil looked around for Penny and heard her voice outside. Harris's men were keeping her at bay.

"Take your controls, ManofNeil," Harris scoffed.

Neil walked up to the game and took his controls, but immediately noticed a slight difference between his bird and Harris's. While Neil's was a standard racing ostrich, it seemed Harris had received a talon upgrade, which increased his speed, handling, and agility during the race.

Of course he cheated. Neil readied himself for the race, taking a few deep breaths. The fate of his friends was riding on this game. At the sound of the horn, the two birds sprinted from their beach starting line into wild jungle, weaving between thick palm trees and ornate slabs of granite. Neil focused intently, keeping an eye on Harris's progress as well as his own. Even with Harris's upgrade, Neil was keeping pace.

"Harris, I gotta say—aside from a few things, this is a pretty fun game," Neil confided. Harris looked dead ahead, saying nothing. "I mean, the marble roll? The racing? I think it's great, and I'm bummed for you it didn't go like you'd hoped."

The two ostriches pushed on, and Neil began pulling ahead by a few yards. Neil leaned forward in concentration.

"Not so fast," said Harris as he grabbed a coconut with his ostrich's mouth and shot it at Neil's bird. Neil's ostrich avatar fell forward, squawking in a comical tumble that sent feathers flying in every direction. Neil rapidly tapped the button on the arcade's console, urging his ostrich to get up and keep running.

"It's the final stretch!" announced the voice of an

ostrich-race announcer, and a racetrack flag flapped across the screen.

Neil gained ground, and as the two ostriches neared the end of the jungle path, he spotted some hidden ostrich-boosting food pellets beneath the shimmering leaves of a plant on the side of the path.

"Pellet power-up!" blasted the game's voice. Neil rocketed forward on the ostrich superfuel, rushing up to Harris's bird. The two furiously ran forward, and Neil could see the finish line just past the edge of the tree line ahead. He slammed every button imaginable, and his bird lunged its long and wiry head forward. It would be a beak-to-beak finish.

"Winner!" shouted the game as an ostrich crossed the finish line. Confetti and streamers rained down on Neil's bird.

"Yes!" Neil yelled, quickly recoiling as Harris slammed his uninjured hand into the console.

"That's impossible . . . ," Harris trailed off.

"Oh, it's possible," Neil said. "But that was a good game. Seriously. I think with a couple of tweaks, this game could go back on the market."

Harris bit his lower lip, deep in contemplation.

"You know what? There's more than one way to reclaim my score," Harris said in anger. He looked behind the speckled arcade system, where the Five-Piece Bandwidth's toolbox was still sitting, long abandoned in the dust behind the Feather Duster console.

"You can always count on those morons to do their jobs poorly," he muttered, sifting through the metal instrument case and pulling out a pair of thick bolt cutters with soft rubber handles and razor-sharp edges. He snipped the padlock and removed the game's metal backing. "Great thing about these machines is the reset function," Harris said as he leaned in and started messing with the inside of the game. Neil noticed the wire cutters on the floor and started to develop a plan.

"There!" Harris exclaimed, victorious. "That ought to do it!" The game made a sad, somber beep as the scores were all reset back to zero. Now no one had the top score.

"Guards," Harris said, nodding at Neil, and the two burly men stepped forward to handcuff him again. They shoved him outside Penny's front doors, and Neil stumbled, nearly losing his balance. He caught himself and turned back for just a second to make eye contact with Penny, who was standing outside, still trying to get into her own pizzeria.

As she and Neil stared at each other, Neil's eyes went wide, in an attempt to say *HELP.*

But only a second passed before Neil was shoved inside the dirty vehicle. They rode back toward the warehouse with Harris in silence. At least this time there wasn't a sack over Neil's face.

They crossed the connecting suspension bridge and pulled into Harris's compound, the doors of the security fence shutting firmly behind them. The car stopped, and Harris led Neil into the makeshift prison with the others.

"Not keeping your side of the bargain?" Neil protested as the guards pushed him inside the room and locked the door behind him. "I won, fair and square!"

"I'm sorry, but I didn't see your name on the high-score card." Harris laughed, then turned and whirled away, talking to himself. "Now to get into wardrobe for the wire transfer."

"Are you serious?" Trevor yelled, trying to jump out of his chair but only succeeding in knocking himself sideways to the ground. Neil winced, but Trevor just kept screaming. "He won! You can't just put him back in prison like that! You promised!"

"It's okay, Trevor," Neil said, reaching out to pull Trevor's chair vertical. He was lucky the guards hadn't taped him to a chair, too—otherwise his new plan would be much more difficult.

"What are you smiling for? You're back in here with us!" Trevor demanded.

"Not for long," Neil said proudly. From the large cargo pocket on the right side of his Five-Piece Bandwidth pants, Neil brandished the wire cutters he'd stolen from the toolbox behind the arcade game while Harris was too distracted to notice.

Neil quickly made the rounds to cut everyone free of their restraints, starting with Jones. The moment Jones's hands were untied, he ripped the duct tape from his mouth and spit a wet clump of sunflower shells onto the floor.

"Grooooosss," Jason 1 and Jason 2 said in unison, then quickly looked away as Jones stared in their direction.

"How long those been in there, Jonesy?" Biggs whispered, his face contorted in disgust. "Surprised those seeds didn't start sprouting from your mouth."

"Nice work, Andertol," Jones croaked, nodding at

Neil and ignoring Biggs.

Neil couldn't help feeling a prickle of pride that he'd done something to impress Jones.

"Now, listen up, recruits. We've got to get out of here." Jones grimaced, rubbing his cheeks where the tape had been. "We're just going to get one shot at this, so we'll need something to distract these jokers."

Neil's eyes immediately flew to the glass panel of their door. They would have to break through it in order to clip their lock to freedom. But the guards were only five feet away—they would come running in an instant.

As his mind raced to create other guesses at an escape plan, Neil heard a commotion coming from the front hallway. A frazzled henchman pushed open the swinging double doors and staggered into the center of the warehouse.

"Fire!" he gasped, wheezing as he bent forward. The other guards in the room rushed over.

"Penny's . . . at Penny's," the sweating guard relayed in broken sentence shards.

"Everyone, I just heard Penny's is on fire!" came another guard, sprinting in from the main hallway.

"You mean the pizza place? You mean the *only* pizza

place!" one of the guards cried out.

"Stop, everyone! You must stop!" yelled the last guard, a feeble-looking man with a squeaky, high-pitched whine. "You're all going to be fired!"

Neil watched as Harris's guards pushed one another out of the way, completely abandoning their outposts, rushing to help protect their precious pineapple pizza.

CHAPTER 23

A SINGLE GUARD STAYED BEHIND, HIS PANICKED EYES DART-ing back and forth. He'd started to run out with the others but hesitated after realizing the warehouse would be left empty. He now paced furiously between the swinging metal doors, the door of the makeshift prison, and the computerized command post in the center of the room.

"Now's our chance. How should we do this?" Neil whispered to the others. Then he locked eyes with Yuri, who nodded. "I know," Neil said. "Let's let the dice decide."

Yuri smiled and produced the twenty-sided die from his pocket. He rolled it on the cold and unforgiving ground.

"We're gonna roll for this? What are we waiting for!" yelled Waffles, who jumped up, his plastic restraints falling to his feet. He grabbed the white die and threw it forcefully at the window of the door. Everyone watched as, in near slow motion, the small projectile ripped through the thin pane, which erupted in a storm of broken glass on the floor of the warehouse.

Dale turned to the sign boasting DAYS WITHOUT INCI-DENT. He erased the *87* printed on it now and replaced it with a big, looping *0*.

The guard turned at the noise, then, his eyes widening, fumbled to grab a radio to communicate with the other henchmen attending to the Great Pizza Fire.

"My lords and ladies, our plan needeth a hero!" shouted a nervous Riley. "Of super proportions!"

Wait. We've got one! thought Neil.

"Jason Two—er, the Shrieking Salamander. Now's your time, buddy!" Neil said, looking directly at Jason 2. Jason looked worried for a second, then nodded and ripped his uniform off in a single motion. Underneath it, he was wearing his sparkly green costume, with a white utility belt clinging around his waist. He ran up to the still-locked doorway and faced the guard, who was running at them fast, fingers fumbling for his weapon.

"Cover your ears, everybody," said Neil. Everyone did, except for Jones, whose bad ear was aimed Neil's way.

"What'd you say? Cover our wha—" Jones started, but an ear-piercing scream rang out before he could finish. It brought Jones to his knees, as well as the guard, who stumbled forward, trying to block out the shrieking noise.

Man, maybe Jason Two really is a superhero, Neil thought.

Jones, his good ear now muffled from Jason 2's scream, grabbed hold of the bolt cutters and reached through the broken window to snip the lock trapping them inside. As it fell to the floor with a thud, Jones pushed open the door, stepping over the broken glass and the shaking guard, who'd been rendered useless.

"We're back in business, everybody," Jones said. "Now, let's get out of here."

"You heard the man, you scum-sucking sacks of grain!" Corinne yelled, doing her best drill sergeant impression. "I want the location of every Chameleon, stat! Let's get out of here—now!"

Following her lead, everyone funneled out of the room and into the hallway toward freedom, swiveling their heads to look for any lingering guards.

"JP!" Corinne was still yelling. "You get your fighter jet and pilots, and I want you off this island in one minute! You got me?"

"Nicely done, pilot," Jones said.

"Our plane," mumbled one of the captured pilots to Neil, his head rolling side to side from exhaustion and Feather Duster prison. "It's over there." He nodded to a remote corner of the warehouse, behind a line of wooden boxes packed full of video games. Neil and Trevor scooped the pilot up on their shoulders and walked toward the corner.

As they slid through a wall of ostrich-themed crewneck sweatshirts, Neil saw a giant open space. He assumed it housed a hidden Chameleon, and on looking closer, Neil saw it wasn't completely invisible. Neil could make out its outline. He walked over and pressed his hand to the plane, breathing a sigh of relief when the hydraulic compartment opened with ease. Since this plane had gone missing before he was entered in the system, he hadn't been a hundred percent sure that it would work.

"I'll take our men with me," Jones said, hoisting the small pilot over his shoulder. Neil glanced to see Wells and Lopez shuffling out with the other captured soldier. "I want to keep a close watch on them. You just get this thing out of here. Andertol"—he looked Neil in the eyes—"why don't you drive?"

Trevor ground his teeth in frustration as he and Neil climbed into the stolen Chameleon. Moments later, they heard three sets of footsteps running toward them.

"Don't think we'll have enough room with everybody out there," said Sam, with Jason 1 at her side. Riley trailed just behind her, doubling over to try to catch his breath. "Mind if we ride with you?"

"Sure thing," said Neil. He was ecstatic. Not only would he get to pilot the fighter, but he'd do it with only his fellow recruits along for the ride, like a real pilot. They huddled in, Jason taking the emergency jump seat.

After buckling himself into the pilot's seat, Neil

started the fighter. "Where's our exit, copilot?" he asked Trevor, reaching for the controls. Trevor pointed directly to the old shipping port shuttered by rusted fencing. "Bingo."

Trevor eased forward on the throttle as the Chameleon slowly began to trample boxes of games and promotional materials. Stuffed ostriches squeaked, then popped, under the tread of the landing-gear tires. The Chameleon accelerated through the confines of the video game warehouse and burst through the gates at the end of the shuttered loading dock. As the nose of the fighter tore through the building, misshapen chunks of chain-link fence shot far into the ocean. They splattered and skipped on the warm surface of the water, thrown out like a handful of skipping rocks.

"Let's see what this baby can do!" Neil shouted as Trevor instinctively pushed forward on the throttle and they took off. The Chameleon skimmed over the glistening water, flying low enough to leave a bubbling wake behind it.

Neil pulled back on the ship's virtual reins, feeling the thrill of gravity pushing down on him as he spiraled upward. His chest throbbing in triumph, he confidently rolled his fighter until they were upside down, covering miles of ocean in mere moments.

"Riley, uh, maketh thine . . . ," Neil stammered, trying to think of words that Riley would understand.

"Prepareth the cloak of un-vision," Sam suggested. Everyone smiled. Suddenly realizing that they were flying without helmets and he needed to be safe, Neil flipped the Chameleon back over and started heading northeast, back toward the *Martin Van Buren*.

"As you wish," said Riley.

But as the Chameleon began activating its scales, something struck Neil as odd. He scanned the altimeter and radar, wondering what was bothering him, but everything was completely normal. Trevor noticed Neil's eyes darting around.

"What are you looking for?" he asked.

"Is something . . . off to you?" Neil asked, keeping firm control of the fighter.

"Not that I'm seeing." Trevor surveyed the cockpit. "Listen, Ashley, don't get paranoid on me now. Relax. You did it, somehow. There's nothing but open sky from here until that ship full of sideburned weirdos."

Neil laughed and shrugged. Maybe Trevor was

right, and he was just overthinking everything. He had done it, after all—he had rescued everyone and was piloting the most top-secret fighter jet in history after freeing it from the clutches of a crazy billionaire. He took a silent moment to let this sink in. And then it struck him.

The buzzing. That high-pitched, Grandma's-house-TV droning that somehow only Neil could hear. He'd heard it on the flight in, but now it was gone. Neil was certain of it. But before he could determine how they'd fix the scales, he was startled by the wailing alarm of the jet's radar.

"Uh-oh," Trevor said. "We've got company."

They turned back to see two jet fighters in hot pursuit. *Do these guys work for Harris, too?* Neil thought. One looked like the same attacker that had harassed them on their flight in. Missiles clung to each craft like suckerfish to a shark. Neil watched as a few warning shots fired past his right wing.

Time to fly.

Without having to say anything, Trevor pushed forward on the throttle. The Chameleon shot forward as if it had been shoved by someone. But the two fighters kept pace, firing shots dangerously close to Neil's wings. Neil expertly dodged back and forth, keeping his jet safe.

"Do they have some kind of radar that can pick us up?" Sam shouted. "They can't see us, but their shots are coming straight for us!"

Neil dipped the controls down, diving toward another small outcropping of rocks. A giant stone arch connected two lush, overgrown islands ahead. Neil pitched his Chameleon and flew closer to the lapping waves below, well beneath the ceiling of the rock bridge ahead.

"Stick with me on this one, Trevor," Neil said to his copilot.

Trevor pushed them faster and faster, streaks of water spouting up in their tailwind.

"So, that split-S move? I'm thinking about a split capital R. Or maybe even one of those German U's with the dots over it. Is that a thing?" Neil asked.

"It is now. Let's do it," Trevor said.

Their fighter threaded through the smooth opening of the arch, leaving plenty of space on all sides. The two bogeys were directly behind them, following intently on their tail.

Neil pulled hard on the controls, looping back until they were upside down, staring at the top of the rock bridge. Neil cranked the controls to his left, and the responsive fighter quickly cut over, slicing down to make another pass.

"Maybe more of a lowercase Q," Neil corrected, his limbs humming as they plunged down to the water below. He swooped back through the arch and heard the sound of the enemy fighter skidding into the water with a splash.

"A pox on that bogey!" screamed an excited Riley.

"You got one!" said Sam. "At least I think that's what he said."

Neil leveled out and flew forward, glancing back to see the second enemy fighter swirl from behind the bubbling wake of its fallen comrade.

"Let's set coordinates for the USS *Martin Van Buren*, everyone," Neil said, hoping to outrun their pursuers and get some muttonchop backup. But before he could even start entering the coordinates, a rocket streaked past the nose of the plane and exploded in bright orange-and-red plumes.

Neil panicked. There was only ocean in front of

them, no other rocks to use for help. It would be a real dogfight, one that might last all the way to the aircraft carrier miles away. Neil's breath grew short, and he slipped back into old habits, wishing for a natural disaster to whisk him out of nervous situations.

Tornado. Lightning bolt. Flash flood. Vol . . .

"Volcano!" yelled Neil. He yanked the plane up and over to head back to the spooky face of the island chain they had just fled.

As the enemy followed in close pursuit, Neil dodged its fire, moving his wings to avoid a targeted missile lock. A bullet barely grazed the right wing, and a frantic siren started up in their cockpit. As the string of islands approached, Neil could see Ostrich Island, where he'd met Weo, and headed for it.

He was flying so low that the tops of palm trees shook and bristled as he jetted past. Behind him, Neil heard the whirling of the enemy's missile targeting system and cringed. They had a lock on him. Just as he reached the lip of the crater, he pulled back, steering clear of the exceedingly hot temperatures of the magma below.

But the Chameleon barely pulled up and began to spin out of control, just the way it had when Trevor had flown over the volcano. Neil struggled to stay firm on the joystick, the plane rattling like the old clothes dryer in his basement. He looked back and saw the enemy jet fly right over the crater. Its wings shimmied violently as the bogey flipped end over end and then turned to head back in the other direction, giving up the chase.

But the Chameleon was still twisting all over the map, flailing like a slow-moving Frisbee. To power out of the revolutions, Trevor slowly pushed the throttle forward. Neil was starting to feel like he was a part of the plane again, just as Jones had said. He tilted the wings, feeling the wind beneath them, almost as if the wings were his own arms. He smoothed the fighter out and triumphantly skimmed just above the whitecaps below.

"Way to go, Neil!" Sam exclaimed. "That was unreal!"

Now the only thing between the recovered Chameleon and the safety of the muttonchop-covered *Martin Van Buren* was a few hundred miles of airborne freedom. Trevor and Neil started to climb to a cruising altitude, guiding the tip of the jet toward the rising sun.

But in the far reaches of his brain, a small, vocal part

- - -

of Neil knew the Chameleon had to stop. *Something is still wrong with this plane.*

"Guys, I . . . I think we have to land. Now," Neil voiced.

"What? No way. Let's just get to the aircraft carrier," Trevor argued.

"Something's wrong with the plane. I can feel it!" Neil insisted.

"Neil, let's just get out of here. What would stopping do?" Jason 1 argued. "If something's wrong, the guys on the *Martin Van Buren* can fix it."

"Sorry, guys," whispered Neil, rearing back in a giant, lightning-fast split S. Trevor tried reaching for the controls, but everyone's weight was magnified by four times that of regular gravity, and Trevor's hand flopped back, useless.

"Come on, come on," Neil muttered. The islands were right below him. Like a futuristic pilot coming out of a light-speed warp drive, Neil pulled back on the jet's thrust. But his timing was off, and he slowed the Chameleon just in time to clip the tops of the tallest palm trees on the island. The nose of the fighter careened down abruptly, burying them once again in the sand.

For the second time this Memorial Day weekend, Neil was at the beach. In the worst possible way.

CHAPTER 24

"IS EVERYBODY OKAY?" NEIL ASKED HIS FLIGHT CREW, RUB-bing the back of his stinging neck.

A muffled "yeah" came from those around him, and Neil breathed a sigh of relief. He looked out the cockpit windows to see ostriches sprinting in every direction. Two strutted up next to the plane and began to peck curiously at the edge of the wing.

"Well, we're back where we started, Ashley. Couldn't get enough of this place, huh?" Trevor groaned. "I can't believe you! We should be halfway to the aircraft carrier!"

Neil tried hovering up and out but only succeeded in creating a clamoring whir of the engines.

"What were you thinking, Neil?" Jason 1 said, sighing.

"And now Harris probably has his communication grid or whatever back up and running," Sam said, defeated. Even she seemed frustrated with him. She flicked the transmission switch for the plane's radio communications, but only static filtered out.

Trevor's barbs were fairly commonplace at this point, but disappointing Sam made Neil feel awful. He'd been so sure something was wrong with the plane, yet maybe he'd acted too soon.

Silently, everyone hopped out of the cockpit to slide down the exterior of the Chameleon and land on the beach. As the others began digging the Chameleon from the sand, Neil turned and faced the water. He needed a minute to think things through and started to skip rocks into the ocean. With every plunk of a rock into the clear-blue water, Neil's thoughts drifted to home and how much he wanted to be there right now, even if Janey had mastered the art of breaking a new type of wood, or whatever roughly femur-sized object she learned to splinter during her weekend tournament.

Hmm, Janey.

When they were little, Janey had once borrowed a working, functioning submarine toy from Neil. It was yellow and remote-controlled, and it was capable of plunging ten feet into the water with ease. Back when he trusted Janey, before she became the terrifying karate enforcer she was today, Neil let her take it to a pool party at a friend's house. It had been one of Neil's favorite toys, but when she returned it, it no longer did anything that made it cool. It didn't dive; it didn't stay upright. He couldn't get it to make even one lousy bubble. Neil was the proud owner of a floating yellow log.

Wait. . . . Neil thought of the dogfight he'd just escaped and how the other planes had always known where they were even though they were invisible. *Could Harris have left the plane for us to take but removed the best part?*

Neil ran back to the Chameleon and crawled into the auxiliary seat. Trevor and Sam were angrily scooping sand from the nose of the fighter, slowly unearthing the craft, while Riley and Jason 1 helped keep away the curious ostriches.

"You feel like helping us, Neil?" Trevor scoffed.

But Neil ignored Trevor, searching instead for the plane's invisibility switch. He turned it on and watched as the plane blinked erratically, trying to turn on the scales. Neil ran back outside, and he could see the exterior as plain as day.

"Guys! Guys! It's the invisibility!" Neil screamed. "That's what Harris wanted! Not the plane. Not us. He took the scales!"

"What are you talking about?" Trevor snapped, but Sam's voice interrupted him.

"Cut it out," she said to Trevor with a glare. "Neil, I'm sorry. What were you saying?"

"The invisibility," Neil explained. "That's why he stole the first plane; that's why he wanted those other fighters. He doesn't care about flying, or the plane. He just wants the invisibility technology."

"Just because you broke our plane's invisibility doesn't mean Harris—" Trevor started to say, but Sam cut him off again.

"Hey, guys," she said, her voice shaking. "I think you'll want to see this."

They turned around and followed her gaze. She

stood transfixed, looking out at Harris's island and the warehouse. They watched as what appeared to be a translucent bubble formed over Harris's island and began shimmering. Slowly, the entire island vanished, fading from the horizon and looking just like another section of roiling seawater against a pastel sky. The suspension bridge from the main island vanished, too.

"He . . . he made the entire *island* invisible," Neil stammered. He looked at his watch, which read 1530H. "We've got thirty minutes till that transfer!"

"We've got to go stop him," Sam said. "The question is, how?"

★ ★ ★

The five kids opened the storage cache for their Chameleon and peered inside, hoping to find something, anything, they could use. In the back corner, Neil spotted a bundle of thick yellow material, which he grabbed and dragged onto the beach.

"Maybe this'll work," Neil said.

Sam hurriedly pulled the inflation valve, and seconds later, a yellow life raft sprang out like a blossoming, waterproof flower. A floating hexagon that could hold them all.

"Okay. Now, let's get in. We've got to get moving," Trevor ordered. He edged the raft toward the water.

"That's the wrong way," Neil and Sam started to say both at once. "The island is that way."

Neil looked up to realize that he and Sam were pointing in completely opposite directions.

"Wait," Sam said, trying to understand what had just happened. "Where is it?"

But no one could agree. Riley and Jason 1 each pointed to different places, too. Somehow, in their haste to come up with a plan, they'd completely lost their sense of direction. It didn't help that everything on the island looked the same, just ostriches and beach and, in the distance, foam-capped waves. Neil tried to search the shoreline for a landmark of some kind, but he saw nothing but more waves and the occasional sandbar.

Wait, that sandbar looks familiar, Neil thought. He examined it more closely, wondering if it was just some memory from being stuck on the island earlier. Then it struck him. Feather Duster! This was the starting line for the final level, the race against Ozzie Tritch. The path that he had followed between sandbars through shallow water and that led all the way to the warehouse. *Harris must have really based the game on this island!*

"Guys, I know this might sound crazy, but I think . . ." Neil hesitated. "I think we need to ride those ostriches." The five of them looked out at the countless birds running across the beach, pecking at whatever bits of food they found on the ground.

"Are you serious?" Sam asked.

"Actually, I am," Neil said, and explained about the game, and how this was the landscape of the final race. "If we can saddle up these bad boys, I'm pretty sure we can ride them to the warehouse."

"I can catch one," Jason 1 said, immediately sprinting after a bird. Neil watched as it sped away from him, irritably flapping its small wings. Neil started to approach one of the ostriches and then remembered Weo's words about the peanut butter sound. He cleared his throat to produce a thick, guttural noise.

"Are you choking?" Sam exclaimed, hurrying forward, ready to administer the Heimlich maneuver.

"No! Weo told me this is how to calm them down. Ostriches, they like the sound of you trying to eat a sandwich with too much peanut butter," Neil explained. He continued, cupping his hands around his mouth while his tongue made a slick, noisy *thwack*.

Trevor started laughing at Neil, but the sound worked—seconds later, a large ostrich was making its way toward Neil, sporadically tilting its head as it moved forward. Neil held his hand out, and the ostrich softly pecked at it, scouring every knuckle for the potential of food.

Riley, who was known in certain regional faire circuits as Ye Olde Swine Whisperer, worked his magic with four other ostriches roaming the beach, gathering them all together into a gray-and-black-feathered ostrich flock.

"Hey there, buddy," Neil murmured, walking up to his ostrich hesitantly. "Wait, sorry. Buddy's a dumb name. I'm going to call you Reggie. Reggie the Ostrich."

The bird squawked in approval.

"Nice. I wish Biggs were here to see this. Something tells me he'd be right at home with this type of thing." Neil placed his left hand on the ostrich's wing and took a huge, bracing hop, swinging his body up onto the flightless bird.

"You guys can do it!" he encouraged the others once he was safely seated on Reggie.

As the others started to jump onto their respective ostriches, Neil experimented with how to control Reggie.

When he pulled gently on Reggie's wings where they connected to his body, the bird pranced in a high-stepping circle. Neil had to focus on balancing or else he would slip right off. As he held on tight using leg muscles that were previously unknown to him, Neil wondered if this was what riding a unicycle was like.

"Okay, guys, let's move," Neil said once everyone was settled. The birds bounced and chortled and flitted around, clearly excited to be moving in a group. "We have to get there by four," he added.

"What happens then?" Sam was leaning completely forward, her arms wrapped tightly around the bony neck of her ostrich.

"To be honest, I'm not sure," Neil admitted. "But we've got to find out."

With a squeeze of his legs, Neil guided Reggie toward the sandbars dotting the horizon. Seeing this, the other ostriches followed, their claws flicking wet sand behind them up in the air. Reggie moved in jagged, huge strides, covering great swaths of ground with ease. The flock headed in the direction of the afternoon sun and slowly curved right, following the thin strips of sand emerging from the water. Neil could feel hot and humid ocean breezes on his face.

"This is nuts!" Sam laughed as she drew even with Neil, their ostriches sprinting ahead. "I'm gonna beat you!"

Jason 1, however, passed both of them, and as the flock sprinted together, they saw a flash of light ahead. It was the edge of the bubble Harris had somehow created. They had unknowingly broken through, and they looked up to see a shimmering bubble encompassing the island.

"Whoa," Neil said as he guided Reggie to step in, then out, then back into the silvery bubble broadcast. It was flawless, almost like being inside a Chameleon. Neil couldn't believe it. Harris had somehow taken the scales and used them to project invisibility so that no one outside the dome could see what was happening within. It was genius.

Trevor's and Riley's ostriches soon caught up, bleating under their weight. They stepped into the bubble and peered back in the direction they'd come from.

"How is he doing it?" Trevor wondered aloud.

Neil swallowed unsteadily. The question wasn't so much *how* as it was *why*. He had to figure out what Harris was plotting.

STILL SITTING ATOP THEIR OSTRICHES, NEIL AND THE OTHERS paused on the wet sand to look at Harris's compound from a new angle. They could see how it was carved into the rock of the island with a tumbling waterfall rushing down its side.

"That's how we get in," Neil said, nodding at the waterfall.

"Wait, you're not serious," Trevor argued.

"Yup. Just trust me. You'll need some speed, and get ready to jump once you break through the water," Neil explained. He felt calm. For the first time in his life, he actually knew what was coming in real life—because he had already played it in a video game.

"I cannot do this," Riley said. "The fall of the waters, I like it not."

"Come on," Trevor snapped, even though just seconds ago he had seemed afraid too.

But Neil was thinking. They didn't *all* need to go inside. And there was something else Riley could do that would help them.

"Riley," Neil said, "do you think you could ride back the way we came?"

"Of course. I can ride for you, my liege," Riley said, bowing his round head in Neil's direction.

"Okay, basically you just need to follow the path we just took and head into the middle of the jungle. Once you pass a rock shaped like an old man's face and see something that looks like it could be called snake mountain, start making noise—a lot of noise. My friend will find you," Neil instructed. "His name is Weo. Tell him Neil needs his help. And keep an eye out for trip wires— he makes one heck of a net."

"I will not let you down, sire!" Riley gushed.

"Fare thee well, Lord Riley," Neil said. Riley smiled and turned to start heading back toward Ostrich Island.

"I'll go with him," said Jason 1. "No way is anybody back home gonna believe this."

"You're sending them to Weo? The kid who held us hostage?" Trevor asked, disbelieving.

"We need backup," Neil said. But that wasn't the whole reason he'd thought of Weo. He remembered the car ride with Harris, how he'd recoiled at the mention of Weo's name. Neil knew that some extra help might be their best chance at stopping him, and Weo and Harris had a history. "Trevor, if you don't want to face the waterfall, you can go back to the other island, too," he offered.

Trevor paused, looking back at the sandy path they'd just traversed, then up at the waterfall. "I'll stay," he said, glaring. "You two wouldn't last long without me. And hey, this is a team, right?"

"You know it. And I'm glad you're on it," Neil responded.

"Whatever."

"All right, let's save the lovey-dovey stuff for the postgame interviews, boys," Sam interrupted, her ostrich restlessly flapping its wings.

Neil turned to face the waterfall again. He took a deep breath, then urged Reggie forward, gathering speed until he was running at the waterfall headfirst. With two more steps, he jerked back on Reggie's bony wings, urging him to leap. With water beading on his feathers, Reggie leaped from one foot over the wide abyss, just like in the video game. Neil peered down and saw magma swirling under thin cracks in the volcanic ground below. *It really is just like the game.*

Neil turned back to make sure the others were okay. He watched as Sam, then Trevor, successfully splashed through the sheet of fast-moving water and over the abyss. Once they had safely joined him, he pivoted to peer down the rocky tunnel, its damp walls echoing the soft, persistent sound of rushing water.

With a nod to the others, Neil dismounted from Reggie and darted off, running down the long, dim tunnel. It wasn't long before he noticed the temperature cooling off, the air growing less damp. And then the tunnel emerged directly into the main room of Harris's warehouse.

Neil stood in a corner of the vast room, blinking in shock at the scene before him.

The warehouse was now barely lit, and dramatic shadows from boxes and equipment were cast down on the floor. Only one of the giant ceiling lights was on, spilling out a single beam. Harris stood on a temporary platform in the center of the room, wearing a skintight silver bodysuit. It literally sparkled, its exterior reflective and metallic. He even wore glasses made of the same material. Around him, his guards stood in a huge pack, all wearing identical costumes. But Neil's eyes were drawn to the object next to Harris, some kind of glowing spire. It looked almost like it could be powering something—*like an island-sized bubble of invisibility, for instance,* he thought. Neil wondered if it could be drawing on the electromagnetic power from the lava below.

"But why sell it now? We could do so many more things!" Neil heard one of Harris's cohorts ask. Neil held out an arm to keep the others back. They still hadn't been seen. "We could rob banks! Take on whole armies!"

"We don't need to rob banks!" Harris exclaimed. "This is just the first two billion dollars. Now that we have the technology, we can clone more of it later. With this money, we'll be one step closer to the grand relaunch. Actually, two billion steps closer."

"But your game got canceled! How are you relaunching?"

Trevor and Sam tiptoed forward, and Neil followed, still utterly silent.

"It'll be easy to relaunch when there are no other games to compete with!" Harris snapped. "As soon as this wire transfer is complete, I will be able to purchase every video-game manufacturer on the planet and destroy them all. I want to eliminate all the competition, and to do that, I'm going to have to go to the source."

"But what will we do when there's no more video games?" a slow-sounding, thick-fingered goon asked.

"You won't need any other games! No one will! Feather Duster and Feather Duster 2: Eclectic Bugaboo are the only games anyone needs! The only games anyone will be able to get!"

"Did . . . are the controls more lifelike?" asked a curious guard.

"The controls are perfect!" Harris yelled shrilly. "You're fired for asking that!"

The giant screen looming behind him, previously blank, lit up with some kind of video chat. Except instead of a face, the square for the other person displayed a red

UNAVAILABLE sign. In the bottom corner of the feed was Harris's face, projecting from where he stood in front of a sleek computer perched atop the control console.

"As promised, before the transfer is complete," Harris said to whoever was on the other end of the video chat, "a look at the technology you're paying for."

"Good," said the gravelly mysterious voice.

Neil noticed that underneath the video chat was a bright-blue progress bar showing the status of a transfer of just over two billion dollars. The progress read 81% and was slowly crawling toward completion. At this rate, it would take only a few minutes to finish.

Harris signaled to a nearby crony, who flipped a switch near the radiant tower in the center of the room. And slowly, just like the Chameleon did and just like the island had, Harris drifted out of sight. Whoever was watching the video feed would be able to see that he was still there as he plopped his white captain's hat onto his invisible head.

"I trust you will find ways of making this useful," Harris said to the person on the other end.

"Oh yes, indeed," said the voice. "And the technology will transfer to me immediately when this monetary transaction is complete? Of course, I wouldn't dream of taking it until the transaction has gone through and you are satisfied."

"Of course," Harris said. "It is programmed to send immediately upon confirmation from my offshore bank."

"Very well," the voice said, and then the transmission ended.

"Guards!" Harris called out, and the same mouth-breathing crony flipped the switch again and returned Harris to a visible state.

"Okay," Neil said, turning back to Sam and Trevor. Both looked as terrified as he did, their faces pale. "You guys heard that, right? What do you think we should do?"

In the corner, Neil could see the now-empty office that they had been held captive in earlier, and his eyes scanned the broken glass as he tried to think of a plan. But then footsteps sounded behind him. Reggie had followed them from the tunnel—and had apparently decided it was time to speak up. He honked loudly, the noise echoing through the warehouse like a fire horn.

At the sound, Harris and his cronies looked up

sharply. "Well, well, well," Harris said. "Look who decided to come back."

With a smirk, Harris reached for the hefty lever on the device next to him. And he and his henchmen all turned invisible.

CHAPTER

26

★ ★ ★

"THEY'VE GONE INVISIBLE!" NEIL SHOUTED, THOUGH HE knew that he was sort of stating the obvious. He lifted his hands in defense, thinking of the way he walked through the frozen-foods section with Janey on the loose: *Always alert. Invisible enemy. Try to momentarily blind her by ripping open a bag of frozen peas.*

Neil moved forward with sporadic and jerky motions, swinging his arms as if they were garden hoses gushing water. His right arm connected with something, so he swung at it, hoping he might actually do some damage, but he couldn't tell what it was. Neil then felt an invisible hand grab his left arm, and he thrashed around, trying to shake off his camouflaged assailant.

Trevor and Sam ran farther out into the main room, punching and kicking into the empty space. But after only a few seconds of battle, invisible arms and hands tugged at their limbs, too. They were immobilized by forces they couldn't see.

"Harris!" Neil shouted.

"Right here, ManofNeil," said a voice in front of Neil.

As Neil scratched and clawed at an invisible guard still holding on to him, the status on the screen above crawled toward completion. Neil kicked in the direction of what he assumed was the guard's pudgy gut and connected, feeling the hands grabbing him release in pain.

"Ninety-two percent!" hollered Trevor.

"Harris, now's your last chance to give up!" Neil shouted. But a kick to his back sent him to the floor. He felt an invisible body pounce on top of him.

"Oh yeah? And who will make me? You and your puny friends?" Harris laughed, an invisible madman. He cranked his arm around Neil's neck and squeezed down tightly. As Neil's cheeks grew red from the pressure, he heard the shouts of his friends being restrained, and an uneasiness washed over him.

Searching for anything, Neil's hands scrambled up to Harris's face. He could feel Harris's glasses. Neil grabbed them and threw them to the ground. Now Harris wouldn't be able to see, either.

"Ah! My glasses!" Harris squealed. The two wrestled and rolled over each other, the blind fighting the blind— or, in this case, the invisible.

Neither of them was exactly a skilled fighter. Unsure of where to attack, they both sliced down with their hands and forearms, occasionally making contact and sending the other into a mad flurry of slaps whenever they did. There was a lot of dramatic yelling and some pinching, but neither of them dared to do too much more.

Keep moving, Neil thought, swiveling his head. But as he bobbed, weaved, and turned to bob again, something connected with his face.

It was the hardest punch Neil had ever taken. Worse than Tommy Scott's. Worse than Janey's. Harris's fist had landed with a spark of pain right on Neil's jaw. Neil dropped to the ground and quickly grabbed his swelling cheek.

- -

For being a code-writing video game nerd, Harris can sure throw a punch, Neil thought. Neil's breath quickened. He looked over to see Trevor being taken out by invisible hands grabbing at him. Sam was being held tight in an invisible bear hug, her legs kicking in the air.

"The download is nearly complete," Harris crowed as he turned Neil's head to the looming screen. "I want you to have a front-row seat for what will happen next."

He felt a tug at his neck as Harris ripped off his dog tags and threw them to the ground. He couldn't believe that after all this, after they'd come so close, he was about to watch as the Chameleon's scales technology fell into some stranger's hands.

But then, in the distance, he heard someone approaching, and it didn't sound like the plodding feet of Harris's goons.

"Verily we ride, my lordship! Onward, my avian brothers and sisters!" Riley's voice amplified down the hallway.

"Who goes there?" Harris shouted in panic, moving away from Neil.

Sitting proudly atop an ostrich and followed by hundreds of other birds, Riley burst through the tunnel and into the warehouse. The hungry ostriches charged ahead and started pecking everywhere for food—including at the blubbery stomachs of invisible guards, who began to squeal and moan in protest.

"Sir Riley," Neil cried out. "You faced the fall of waters."

"It was all thanks to my trusty steed, the noble Bartholomew," Riley replied, gesturing to his ostrich. "And I am but a humble squire, my lord, joined in pursuit with Sir Jason the First."

Jason 1 bowed from atop an ostrich, then sprang off to try to help his captured friends.

"Here is Sir Weo, whose assistance you requested," Riley finished, heading after Jason to help him pry open the arms of the guards holding Sam and Trevor.

"You okay there, Neil?" Weo asked, staring down at Neil, who was still on the ground. Weo was sitting on the tallest ostrich of all, in a specially made ostrich saddle.

"Weo!" Neil cried out.

"Guards, attack him!" commanded Harris, but they were all too busy fighting off the persistent birds.

"The switch! That thing right over there—flip it!" Neil yelled to Weo before he felt Harris's boot on his face.

Weo charged his bird ahead, dodging invisible guards as he made his way to the switch. With a quick flip, Harris and his men became visible.

"Harris, stop it," demanded Weo, his eyes flying to where Harris stood over Neil.

From the ground, Neil watched the status of the transfer inching along. While the money's destination was encrypted on the screen, Neil knew that once it was complete, it would mean that the most advanced camouflaging technology in the world would be in the hands of some anonymous and possibly dangerous stranger.

"And why should I listen to someone who just abandons his friends?" Harris snorted, still pinning Neil to the ground. Around him, ostriches chased his goons, but he ignored them.

"Weo!" Neil interrupted. "We've got to stop this transfer. Harris is selling the invisibility technology from our jet, and it cannot fall into the wrong hands. It's top secret!"

Harris rapped Neil on the back of his head, and Neil gritted his teeth.

"Your *jet*?" Weo asked. "Scientists get jets?"

Neil had nearly forgotten that Weo didn't know the

truth. "Well, I know it might not look like it, but I'm with the Air Force. The US Air Force," Neil explained. Weo looked shocked.

"It's true!" cried Trevor, who broke free of one grasp only to be clotheslined by another. He dropped below a small flock of ostriches.

"Wow, I'm surprised they let you guys in. Do they have physical requirements these days, or are they just taking anybody?" Weo ribbed. "It's okay. I mean, chameleon-hunting scientists? I kind of knew there was something fishy going on." He hopped off his ostrich and walked over to Harris.

"Is this true? Why would you have to steal something and sell it? What happened to the money from the game?"

"You know they pulled the game," Harris said. Then he grew quieter. "After you left, the game turned awful. The controls got all weird. The controls that only you knew, and only you could help with."

Watching Harris talk to Weo, Neil didn't think he seemed like a truly evil villain at all. He seemed almost vulnerable.

"It was what you deserved after you fired my father," Weo replied.

"My father said we had to cut spending somewhere. I fought him all the way!" Harris said in defense.

"I don't believe you!" Weo shot back. "I'm glad I didn't help finish your stupid controls! I'm doing just fine on my island without you."

Clearly, Neil thought, there was bad blood between them, the kind that had apparently escalated to net-capturing lengths.

"Hey, guys?" Neil said, his face still smushed on the cold concrete floor. "How about this: Weo, what would it take for you to come back and help with the second Feather Duster?" Neil's eyes watched the download percentage click to 99% and the lettering turn to a bright and serious red. There was probably a minute or so remaining before the technology was gone for good.

"He knows," Weo said, glaring at Harris.

"Harris, I think you know what that means. If Weo came back to help with your game, is there a job left for his father?"

Harris didn't respond, only sat motionless. Neil

watched as guards grouped together, having now wrangled in all of Neil's fellow recruits.

"Harris, you can stop this and relaunch your game—the right way. Don't you want everyone buying it because they love it? Not because it's the only option they have available?" Neil could feel the tension of Harris's grip growing looser. "Listen," he pressed on. "I'm not the one who pulled your game, and neither is Weo. And things aren't ruined yet. But they're about to be. Now, let me help you before you get into actual, serious trouble. Let's stop this together."

Harris eased off but still drove a knee into Neil's back, keeping him immobilized.

"Weo, that laptop," Neil cried out, giving up on Harris. "Go to that laptop! There's got to be a kill code we can enter!"

Weo hurried over to the silvery notebook open on the control console, the guards seemingly hesitant to attack him. Neil realized they all must have worked with Weo's father.

"You forgot to use those motion-sensor thingies," Weo said tentatively to Harris, glancing at him from behind the computer. Neil eyed the final percentage of the download, a lump forming in his throat. "We could get some of those. They could help. But only if you'll help me."

Harris was silent, his body heaving as he still stood over Neil.

"HnWFriends4Ever," Harris whispered.

"What?" Weo asked.

"Our code! Enter it!" Harris responded. Weo typed it into the computer, and the screen froze. Neil feared it was too late. Weo hit ENTER twice more, and a giant *X* appeared, refreshing the page and replacing the status bar.

Seconds later, a scrambled video feed flashed on the giant screen.

"What's going on?" screamed the mystery man expecting the invisibility technology. "You can't cancel on me! You promised me that software! Give it to me, *now*!"

"Sorry," Harris said, stepping forward into the video chat window. Neil, at last able to move his neck, started to sit up. "I changed my mind," Harris said, and hung up the call.

Free from Harris's grip, Neil walked toward the dock to stretch out when from above he heard a whirring sound approaching. *The Chameleons operating in humidity!* Neil remembered.

"Back up!" Neil yelled to everybody in anticipation of a jet's arrival, and after a whoosh of air passed over him, he knew it had landed.

Like a bead of quicksilver, the craft slowly glimmered into visibility, and the cockpit lid opened. Jones and Lopez jumped out.

"Andertol! We tried to radio you! When we didn't hear from you, we circled back, only to find this whole place flickering in and out like a giant hologram!" Jones shouted. He turned to Harris, who was standing near the laptop, his hands in the air. "You! Stay back!"

"I surrender! I surrender!" exclaimed Harris, closing his eyes as if bracing himself for the worst.

Jones took a step forward, then suddenly slipped on something black on the floor, landing on his rear end. He sat up slowly, glaring at Harris, who looked like he might faint.

"Sorry," Harris said, his voice small. "That's the Feather Duster–themed ostrich ooze. Limited edition. It should come right off with the Feather Duster screen wipe pads. You'll find them right up there, in that box in the far corner." Harris gestured with his chin, still clearly scared to lower his arms and point.

Jones frowned and got back to his feet, his eyes still on Harris. "Okay, kid," he said. "Who are you, and what did you do to my missing Chameleon?"

"My name is Harris Beed. I design video games. Well, just one video game, and its sequel," Harris babbled to Jones. "I'll return your stolen invisibility technology. I promise." He looked right at Weo. "You can trust me."

★ ★ ★

Neil stood with the rest of the team in the sun-soaked courtyard of the compound, waiting to take off for the aircraft carrier. Harris, handcuffed, stood next to Jones while the major furiously wrote some kind of mission report on an official-looking Air Force pad. Penny was there and milled around, handing out small slices of pineapple pizza. The twelve starving gamers quickly finished them off.

"I thought your place burned down?" Neil asked her, grabbing a thin slice. He was hooked.

"Just that silly video game caught fire, Mr. Plain Cheese," she said with a smile. "Must have happened when Harris messed around with those scores."

Finishing his bite, Neil spied Jones leaving Harris, who looked dejected, his hair falling in front of his face as he stared somberly at the ground. Neil walked over to him.

"Harris," said Neil.

"Yeah? What do you want?" Harris looked up at him in surprise and confusion.

"Just . . . here's my username, if you ever want to play, once—well, once whatever happens, happens," Neil said, extending a crumpled piece of paper. Harris didn't move to take the paper, so Neil laid it by his feet and began to walk toward his Chameleon, now dug out of the sand of Ostrich Island.

"Hey, Neil!" yelled Harris. Neil stopped in his tracks, spinning around. "You meant what you said before? That you liked the game?"

"Yeah," Neil replied. "I really did. Although having done the real thing, you may want to get some of those motion-sensor devices, like Weo said. Just so players can get the feel for it. I mean, it's a rush."

"Yeah, it is, isn't it," Harris said, looking into the distance fondly. "You know, I just might."

"Harris, my man," Biggs said, approaching him.

"Let's say, hypothetical situation: You have created a video game that proclaims you'll even *smell* like an ostrich. And then there's a gentleman who, I don't know, has created a smell journal for the long journey humans are about to take into smellable television. And this gentleman may happen to"—Biggs winked—"*know* people."

Harris turned to Biggs. "You know? Hypothetically speaking, we might just be able to look into that," he replied.

Jones glanced up from his paperwork and rolled his eyes. "Come on, Andertol," he said, leading Neil out into the middle of the courtyard. The glowing light of an island sunset seeped down around them. The grass was springy under their boots. "Andertol, I just wanted to say—well, I wasn't too sure about you at first, but you're all right. Now, let's get those Chameleons fired up. We've got to get home. Recruits!" Jones called out, then seemed to think better of it. "Soldiers! Time to move out!

"And Andertol," Jones added. "How about you fly the stolen bird?"

Neil nodded. "Sir, yes, sir." Neil saluted, then lingered as Jones headed back toward Harris. He was curious about what Harris's punishment would be. Despite all that had happened, he hoped that everything with Harris would end up okay.

"Now, Harris," he heard Jones say, "if I didn't love that stupid ostrich game of yours, you'd be in serious trouble. So I've got some special plans for you." Jones cracked his knuckles and rolled his neck with a satisfying pop. "You're going to tell me everything I need to know. The first thing being the location of that blasted talon upgrade. Now, get up. I'm not a babysitter."

CHAPTER

27

AS NEIL FLEW HIGH INTO THE ENDLESS SKY, HE REFLECTED ON all that Jones had told him about flying. He pitched and yawed, and it felt like he was swimming underwater, like the plane was part of his own body once again.

"Nice," said Neil's copilot. He was one of the men they'd been sent to rescue. The other, exhausted, had slumped in one of the backseats.

Neil let out a yawn, realizing how little sleep he'd had over the past two nights. As his steering began drifting, the copilot leaned forward.

"Mind if I—" he asked.

"Oh, thanks. I can keep go*waaahhh*—" Neil started, but another yawn took control. "Okay, yeah. Maybe a break for a few minutes. But don't think you're landing this puppy."

"I'm impressed, kid. Glad to see they went ahead and declassified the program to let you kids fly," said the pilot in the back.

"Oh, nothing was classified, really. Was it?" Neil said, beginning to drift into the comforting riptide of a little shut-eye.

"You mean they didn't tell you about Level Twelve?"

Neil shook his head, his eyelids slowly batting. The pilot pointed to the patch on his left sleeve. Where Neil's was embroidered with the seal of the Air Force, this pilot had an entirely different patch. It read LEVEL TWELVE in a half circle below a shadowy Earth. In one motion, the sleepy pilot in the auxiliary seat ripped the patch from his own sleeve, then reached forward and placed it in Neil's palm. The pilot's hand soon dropped to the floor as he fell into a deep sleep.

"Don't worry about him. He hasn't slept since Thursday," said Neil's copilot.

--

Wow, I can't believe it's only been a weekend. It would soon be Monday—and Neil's family would be home. He tried to imagine what type of karate podium Janey was currently standing on and then quickly nodded off for a minute. He started into an elaborate dream where he was yet again the hero, but his eyes opened. *I'm living this dream now. Save the sleep for later.*

Neil watched the aircraft carrier appear on the Chameleon's radar and calmly guided the fighter onto the deck of the USS *Martin Van Buren*. He reached up to grasp the dog tags clinging around his neck, dragging his thumb over the raised letters.

The sun dipped farther into a bed of clouds, and the sky was a fading orange as the cockpit slid open. Excited muttonchop soldiers gathered around, shouting and talking over one another.

The sailors of the *Martin Van Buren* grabbed Neil, unfastening his safety restraints and crowd-surfing him to the boat deck. Neil smiled as people of all ranks came out to voice their appreciation.

"Let's get a grandfather clause for that haircut, too!" shouted a voice from the top deck of the aircraft carrier. Everyone laughed as Neil reached up to touch the haircut he'd almost forgotten about.

Neil spied Sam standing near the edge of the aircraft carrier and asked for everyone to set him down. After a few high fives, he walked over to her. Her dark hair was twirling in the wind. The two stood there for a moment in silence, looking at the sun as it began to duck into the horizon for the night. A few stars popped into view.

"See that? That's Sasquatch Minor," Neil joked, pointing to some barely visible specks in the sky. Sam smiled, and Neil felt comfortable.

"Here, I want you to have this," Sam said, offering him her lucky trilobite from her pocket. "Just in case you need good luck or anything."

"I can't take your good luck charm!" Neil argued, moving his hand away from Sam's.

"Come on, just take it," she insisted, grabbing his hand and pushing the trilobite into his crinkled palm. "I found an ostrich talon on the beach, so I think that's a sign that it's time to swap anyway. Might even look into getting an eighteenth favorite thing."

They chuckled. "Samantha?" someone called from behind them. "You're wanted on the flight deck for departure."

Sam sighed. "I guess this is good-bye for now," she said. "See you online, ManofNeil?"

"Of course," Neil replied. They hugged quickly, and it somehow wasn't weird at all.

"Time to get a move on, soldiers. Your weekend's almost up, and we've got some curious parents making calls," barked a soldier with shorter, five o'clock–shadow chops. "Who's Hurbigg? We need you to come in and shoot a video for your mom. She's apparently tried to call your cell eighty-seven times since yesterday morning."

There, on an aircraft carrier in the middle of the ocean, they all gathered to say good-bye. Jason 2 in his costume, sharing contact information with Jason 1. Yuri proudly saluting, the 13 on his white, now-misshapen die proudly facing outward. Corinne spelling out *USA* in grandiose body movements. Dale and Waffles gyrating in an attention-deficit dance. And then there was Trevor, who was, just barely, smiling at Neil.

Soon they would all go their separate ways, taking commercial flights home to avoid any suspicion. Neil didn't know when he'd see everyone again, but he would miss them all. Then again, they were all just an internet connection away.

Neil turned to follow Jones and begin the long trip home but realized he hadn't said a proper good-bye to Biggs. Neil spotted him across the deck, sitting in front of a green screen while some of the *Martin Van Buren* soldiers were slumped over a laptop.

"Okay, kid!" Neil heard the soldier shout. "We told your mom you were at camp, so just read this card, and we'll be that much closer to getting you home."

"Dear Mom. Camp is great. I'll be home early Monday," Biggs said, but paused and went off script for his next line. *"Feed the cats!"*

★ ★ ★

Monday evening, Neil sat in the backseat of a hired limousine. It was long and fancy. The driver had been at the airport waiting for him, holding a sign with Neil's name on it. Neil leaned back into the seat and started to eat the airplane snacks he'd taken from the flight. This was the life.

He was well on his way to eating his weight in pretzels when the car rolled up in front of his house. He thanked the driver and headed up to his garage door, wondering if anyone was home. He stood on his toes to peer in the window, his hands circling around his eyes to fight the sun's glare. The garage was empty: his mom and Janey still hadn't returned from the tournament.

Neil grabbed the spare key from underneath a fake rock and slipped through his back door. After everything that had happened over the last few days, it felt strange to be home. He hurried upstairs to his room to turn on Chameleon out of habit and smiled. Sam's icon popped up on Neil's screen at the same moment, his speakers making the little bubbling noise Neil had set to alert him whenever Sam signed on. It felt just like before. The only difference now was— *Well, there are a lot of differences now,* Neil thought. *But in the best way.*

Welcome home, ManofNeil! Sam sent in a message that flashed across his screen. He smiled.

Can't play now, he wrote back. *C U later?*

Neil wandered slowly downstairs, his attention drawn to the family's mantel. He removed the entries occupying his side and placed Sam's trilobite there, along with the patch the rescued pilot had given him. He heard a beep in the other room and walked over to play the voice mail message waiting for the Andertols.

"Hi, guys. It's Mrs. Scott. Tommy said he called

already but glad to hear Neil's friend's mom was able to come pick him up. I think the other boys really loved having him around, if he'd ever like to—"

"You have no new messages," said a robot voice as Neil pushed delete with a smirk. For once Neil appreciated Tommy Scott and his dense brother, even though Tommy had clearly only been lying to save himself.

Suddenly Neil heard the sounds of his mom arriving home, the metal planks of the garage door rolling up their smooth metal track. He turned to see Janey swing open the door connecting the garage to the kitchen. She was still wearing her white karate gear, and three yellow-banded medals hung around her neck. In her left hand, she held a trophy shaped like a hand chopping a giant evergreen tree.

"Neil! First place!" she screamed, punching a decorative basket of fake flowers off the stone countertop with her free hand.

"Nice job, Janey!"

He reached out his hand for a high five. Janey looked puzzled, not sure whether this was actual encouragement or if her brother had been replaced by a robot.

"Hi, honey," said Neil's mom. She walked through the

garage doorway, her arms filled with bags of clothes and the watered-down remnants of an iced coffee. "You have a good weekend at Tommy's? I was surprised not to get a call from you all weekend. You must've been having so much fun!"

"Erh, yeah. Yeah, something like that. It was a really great weekend," Neil said with a smile.

"That's great. We're both starved. Can you order pizza, Neil?" Mrs. Andertol asked, pushing her sunglasses to the top of her head.

"Sure thing," Neil replied. He went to the cordless phone in the kitchen and began to order. "Hi, delivery, please? Thanks. We'd like an extra-large pizza. Extra pineapple."

Neil's mother stopped in her tracks as if she had just heard a criminal confession.

"Neil, are you okay?" she asked, feeling his forehead with the back of her hand while he gave the pizza place their address.

"Never been better!" he said, hanging up the phone. "Have you never had pineapple pizza before, Mom? You really need to expand your horizons. I'll be upstairs if you need me."

He climbed the stairs two at a time and returned to his room. Sam had signed off, but a new message blinked in its place.

User HarrIsTheBest has sent you a message.

The message consisted of a simple line of text with attachments. *Neil—Thanks for your help. Enjoy.*

Attached were Feather Duster and the anticipated sequel—Feather Duster 2: Eclectic Bugaboo (Beta). Neil opened the new game and saw the menu screen. Since it wasn't an official game yet, the wallpaper showed a picture of Harris and Weo. They each sat atop an ostrich, green motion-sensor balls stuck to their birds' legs, wings, heads, and tails.

Neil selected the game, and the screen flashed to life with the plumage and chortling of an ostrich. A warning message appeared, alerting the user that since this was still in demo-only mode, options for a cartridge with a smellable experience were still unavailable.

As Neil selected his ostrich, which came with a new naming option, the doorbell rang downstairs.

"Whoa, that was quick," he said, pausing the game before rushing down the steps. He flung open the front door only to hear the squeak of tires. A black SUV was pulling away, turning the corner at the end of his street. Instead of the pizza he was expecting, a white envelope sat on the doorstep. Neil picked it up and examined it closely, running his finger over the logo for NASA printed on the thick white paper. Neil turned it over. TOP SECRET: FOR N. ANDERTOL ONLY was scrawled on the back.

Neil shut the door and raced back upstairs, locking himself in his room before sliding his forefinger through the adhesive closure. The envelope contained an un-labeled black CD and a note. Quickly fumbling with the buttons on his console, Neil popped open the drive and inserted the disc. The screen opened with a rocket, much like a Chameleon, hurtling through black and starry outer space. Swirls of stars and galaxies were bursting out in every direction.

Neil looked down at the note. The writing was in all capital letters, written in fountain pen.

Nice work, Andertol. I wanted to write you personally to say so. We probably wouldn't be alive without you. You should feel good about that. But now I get a summer with the grandkids . . . babysitting. Go figure. Anyway,

--

thought you should have this. Keep practicing.
You never know when we may need you again.
—*Major Clancy Shannon Jones.*

Neil looked up at the screen and smiled. He grabbed his controller and confidently pressed PLAY.

ACKNOWLEDGMENTS

A huge thank-you to the folks at Alloy and HarperCollins for making this series possible. First, my brilliant editors: Katie McGee, for her encouragement and direction, and Rachel Abrams for her invaluable insight and notes.

Joelle Hobeika, for her incomparable support and ability to tolerate years of ridiculously unprofessional emails. And many thanks to Josh Bank for the opportunity.

I am thoroughly grateful for the unending support I've received from my family and friends. I appreciate you all, and promise I will get better at keeping in touch.